BLOOD DEBT

"I hear tell they call you Smoke and that you're lookin' for me," the barrel-chested rancher said. "If so, here I am."

"News to me," Smoke said. "What's your name?"

"You know who I am, kid," he snarled. "Ackerman."

"Oh, yeah!" Smoke smiled thinly. "You're the man who shot my brother in the back and then stole the gold he was guarding."

"You're a liar. I didn't shoot your brother; that was Potter and his bunch."

"You stood and watched it. Then you stole the gold."

"It was war, kid."

"But you were on the same side," Smoke said. "So that not only makes you a killer, it makes you a traitor and a coward."

"I'll kill you for sayin' that!"

"You'll burn in hell a long time before I'm dead," Smoke said tightly.

Ackerman grabbed for his pistol. . . .

THE LAST MOUNTAIN MAN

By William W. Johnstone

ZEBRA BOOKS
KENSINGTON PUBLISHING CORP.

To Jon Burchardt

ZEBRA BOOKS

are published by

Kensington Publishing Corp.
475 Park Avenue South
New York, N.Y. 10016

Sixth printing: June, 1990

Printed in the United States of America

We were victims of circumstances. We were drove to it.

Cole Younger, 1876

Author's note: The mountains and valleys and creeks and springs described in this novel are real. The rendezvous of aging mountain men at Bent's Fort reportedly did take place around 1865. The grave with the gold buried alongside the man supposedly exists, but it is not at Brown's Hole. To the best of my knowledge there is no town in Idaho called Bury. The story is pure Western fiction, and any resemblance to actual living persons is purely coincidental.

PROLOGUE

He was sixteen when his father returned from that bloody insurrection known to the North as the Civil War. The War Between the States to those who wore the gray.

Kirby Jensen was almost a man grown at sixteen, for he had worked the farm during his father's absence, taking over all the work when his mother fell ill and was confined to bed.

And it had been backbreaking work, attempting to scratch a living out of the rocky Ozark Mountain earth of southwestern Missouri. There never was enough food. The boy was thin, but rawhide tough, for the work had hardened his muscles and the pure act of survival had sharpened his mind. His hands were large and calloused from using an axe, handling trace chains on the mule team, and manhandling rocks from the rolling acres of land he, and he alone, had farmed since age twelve.

It was June, 1865, the war had been over and done for better than two months. If his father was coming home, he should be along anytime, now. *If* he was coming home.

Kirby wondered what his Pa would say when he learned his daughter had run off with a peddler? He wondered if he knew his oldest boy was dead? And he wondered what his reaction would be when Kirby told him of Ma's dying?

The plow hit a rock and jolted the boy back to his surroundings, popping his teeth together and wrenching his arms.

The boy swore. Made him feel more grown-up to cuss a little.

He unhooked the plow, running the lines through the eyes of the singletree, and left the plow sitting in the middle of the field. He was late getting the crops in, but no later than anyone else in the hollows and valleys of this part of Missouri. The rains had come, and stayed, making field work impossible. But he had to try to get something up.

It was a matter of survival.

Folding and shortening the traces, Kirby jumped on the back of one of the big Missouri Reds, the one called Ange, and kicked the mule into movement. It really didn't make any difference how much you kicked ol' Ange, for the mule would prod along at its own pace, oblivious to the thumping heels in its side. But if you kicked too much, ol' Ange would dump a body on his butt, then stand over you and bray, kind of like mule laughter. Made you feel like a fool.

Then you had a devil of a time getting back on Ange.

Kirby plodded down the turn row on the east side of the field. Dust from the road caught his eyes. One rider pulling up to the house, leading a saddleless, riderless horse. A bay. The boy touched the smooth butt of the Navy .36 stuck behind his wide belt. A man just couldn't be too careful these days, what with some of those Kansas Jayhawkers still around, killing and looting and raping. But, he reminded himself, some of the Missouri Redlegs were just as bad as the Jayhawkers. Seems like war brought out the poison in some and the good in others.

Kirby's father hadn't held much with slavery, but he did feel a state had a right to set and uphold its own laws, so he had ridden off to fight with the Gray. His Pa's brother, up in Iowa, whom Kirby had not seen but one time in his life, was a farmer, like most of the Jensen men. But he had marched off to fight with the Blue. He had gotten killed, so Kirby had heard, in Chancellorsville, back in '63.

At sixteen, Kirby didn't believe a man had the right to keep another in chains, as a slave, although there hadn't been much of that in this part of Missouri: everybody was too poor, just a day to day struggle keeping body and soul together.

But he did believe, like this father, probably because of his father, that the government in far-off Washington on the river didn't have the right to tell a state what it could and couldn't do in *all* matters.

Didn't seem right.

Had Kirby been old enough, and not had his Ma to look after, he would have ridden for the Gray.

As Ange plodded closer to the house, Kirby could make out the figure in the front yard. It was his father.

ONE

"Boy," Emmett Jensen said looking at his son, "I swear you've grown two feet."

Kirby had slid off Ange and walked to the man. "You've been gone four years, Pa." He wanted to throw his arms around his Pa, but didn't, 'cause his Pa didn't hold with a lot of touching between men. Kirby stuck out his hand and his Pa shook it.

"Strong, too," Emmett commented.

"Thank you, Pa."

"Crops is late, Kirby."

"Yes, sir. Rains come and stayed."

"I wasn't faultin' you, boy." Emmett let his eyes sweep the land. He coughed, a dry hacking. "I seen a cross on the hill overlookin' the creek. Would that be your Ma?"

"Yes, sir."

"When'd she pass?"

"Spring of last year. Doc Blanchard said it was her lungs and a bad heart." And grief, the boy thought, but kept that to himself.

"She go hard?"

"No, sir. Went on in her sleep. I found her the next morning when I brung her coffee and grits."

"Good coffee's scarce. What'd you do with the coffee?"

"Drank it," the boy replied honestly. "Then went to get the doc."

"Right nice service?"

"Folks come from all over to see her off."

Emmett cleared his throat and then coughed. "Well, I think I'll go up to the hill and sit with your ma for a time. You put up them horses and rub them down. We'll talk over supper."

Emmett's eyes flicked over the .36 stuck behind his son's belt. He said nothing about it.

"Pa?"

The father looked at his son.

"I'm glad you're back."

The father stepped forward, put his arms around his son, and held him.

Over greens and fried squirrel and panbread, the father and son ate and talked through the years that they had both lost and gained. There were a few moments of uncomfortable silence between them until they both adjusted to the time and place, and then they were once more father and son.

"We done our best," Emmett said. "Can't nobody say we didn't. And there ain't nobody got nothing to be ashamed of. I thought it wrong for the Yankees to burn folks' homes like they did. But it was war, and terrible things happen in war. But the bluebellies just kept on comin'. Shoot one and five'd take his place. They weren't near 'bout the riflemen we was, nor the riders, but they whipped us fair and square and now it's time to put all that behind us and get on with livin'." He sopped a piece of panbread through the juice of his greens. He chewed for a time. "You know your brother, Luke, is dead, don't you?"

"Yes, sir. I didn't know if you did, or not. I heard he was killed in the Wilderness, last year. Fightin' with Lee, wasn't he?"

Luke had always been Pa's favorite, so Kirby had felt.

Emmett nodded. "Yeah. Tryin' to get back to the Wilderness, so I heard." Something in his eyes clouded, as if he knew more about his son's death than he was telling. "I don't see no sign of your sister, Janey, and you ain't brought up her name. What are you holding back, Kirby?"

The moment the boy had been dreading. "She run off, Pa. Last year. Run off with a tinker, so he called himself. But he was a gambler, I'd say."

"Smooth-talker, I'd wager."

"Yes, sir."

"What'd his hands look like?"

"Soft."

"Gambler. How'd your Ma take it?"

"Hard."

"Probably helped kill her." He said it flatly, then shook his head. "Well, past is past, no point dwellin' on it." He rose from the table. "I've ridden a piece these last weeks—wanted to get home. Now I'm home, and I'm tired. Reckon you are, too, son. We'll get some sleep, talk in the morning. I got a plan." He covered his mouth and coughed.

* * *

Breakfast was meager: fried mush and coffee that was mostly chicory. A piece of leftover panbread.

"I don't think it good to stay here, boy," Emmett said, surprising the boy. "Too many memories. Land's got too many rocks to farm. I think it best for us to pack it up, sell what we can, and head west. We'll sell the mules, buy some pack horses. The mules is gettin' too old for where we're goin'. What is today, boy?"

"Wednesday, Pa." *West!* he thought. The frontier he'd read about in the dime novels. Buffalo and mountain men. Then he sobered as he thought: *Indians on the warpath.*

Emmett pushed his plate from him and put his elbows on the table. "We'll ride into town today, boy. Ask around some. Kirby, I brought that bay out yonder home for you."

Kirby mumbled his thanks, pleased but embarrassed. He had never had such a grand gift.

"How far you been from this holler, boy?"

"A good piece, Pa. I went to Springfield once. Took us a good bit of travelin' to get there, too."

Seventy miles.

Emmett stuffed his pipe and lit it, then pushed his rawhide-bottomed chair back and looked at his son. "Toward the end of the war, Kirby, some Texicans and some mountain men joined up with us. Them mountain men had been all the way to the Pacific Ocean; but they talked a lot about a place the Shoshone Indians call I-dee-ho. Or something like that. I'd like to see it, and all the country between here and there. I been all the way to the Atlantic Ocean, boy—you never seen so much water. You just got no idea how big this country is. But west is where the people's got to go. I figure we'll just head on out that way, too."

"Pa? How will we know when we get to where it is we're goin'?"

"We'll know," the man replied, a mysterious quality to his voice, as if he was holding back from his son.

Kirby met his father's eyes. "Whatever you say, Pa."

They pulled out the following Sunday morning, just as the sun was touching the eastern rim of the Ozark Mountains of Missouri. Kirby rode the bay, sitting on a worn-out McClellan saddle; not the most comfortable saddle ever invented. The saddle had been bought from a down-on-his-luck Confederate soldier trying to get back to Louisiana.

In Kirby's saddlebags, in addition to an extra pair of trousers, shirt, long handle underwear, and two pairs of socks, a worn McGuffey's reader his Pa had purchased for a penny—much to Kirby's disgust. He thought he was all done with schooling.

The boy had no way of knowing that his education was just beginning.

The McGuffey's reader was heavy on his mind. As they rode, he turned to his father. "I can read and cipher." He knew his protests would fall on deaf ears. Once his father made up his mind, forget any objections . . . just do it.

"I 'spect you can," Emmett said, his eyes still on the little valley below them. His eyes lifted, touching the now tiny cross on the faraway knoll. He touched his boot heels to his mount and father and son headed west. "What's a verb?"

Kirby looked at him. "Huh? I mean, sir?"

"A verb, boy. Tell me what it is."

Kirby frantically searched his memory. "Well," he admitted. "Reckon I forgot. You brung it up, so you tell me."

"Don't sass me, boy." But there was a twinkle in the father's eyes. "I asked you first."

"Then I reckon we'll find out together, Pa."

"I reckon we will at that, boy." Emmett turned once, twisting in the saddle to look for the last time at the cross on the knoll. He straightened in the saddle, assuming the cavalryman's stiff-backed position. He asked his son, "You got any regrets, Kirby? Leavin' this place, I mean."

"Hard work, not always enough food, Jayhawkers, Yankees, cold winters, and some bad memories," the boy replied honestly, as was his fashion. "If that's regrets, I'm happy to leave them behind."

Emmett's reply was unusually soft. "You was just a boy when I pulled out with the Grays. I reckon I done you and your Ma a disservice—like half a million other men done their loved ones. I didn't leave you no time for youthful foolishness; no time to be a young boy. You had to be a man at twelve. I don't know if I can make up for that, but I aim to try. From now on, son, it'll be you and me." For a little while, he silently added. He coughed.

Together they rode, edging slightly northward as

they went. They skirted Joplin, a town on the Ozark plateau. It was a young town, only twenty-five years old in 1865. Joplin had a few years to go before it would become the metropolis of a three-state lead and zinc field. Kirby wanted to ride in and see the town, the only other big town he'd ever seen was Springfield. But his father refused, said there were dens of iniquity in there.

"What's a den of in . . . in . . . what'd you say, Pa?"

"You'll find out soon enough, I reckon."

"Why don't you tell me, Pa?"

"'Cause I ain't of a mind to, that's why." The father seemed embarrassed.

"Sure must be something pretty danged good."

Emmett smiled. "Some folks would say so, I'm sure. Never been to one myself. And don't cuss. It ain't seemly and you might slip and do so around a lady. Ladies don't like cussin'."

"You say hell's fire, Pa," he reminded.

"That's different."

"How come?"

"Boy, you sure ask a lot of questions. Worrisome."

"Well, how else am I to learn?"

"I can cuss now and then 'cause I'm older than you, that's why."

"How long will it be 'fore I can cuss, Pa?"

The father shook his head and hacked his dry cough. "Lord have mercy on a poor veteran and give me strength." But he was smiling as he said it.

They had left the cool valleys and hills of Missouri, with rushing creeks and shade trees. They rode into a hot Kansas summer. Only four years into the Union, much of Kansas was unsettled, with almost the entire western half the territory of the Kiowa and Pawnee; the Kiowa to the south, the Pawnee to the north.

The pair rode slowly, the pack horses trailing from lead ropes. The father and son had no deadline to meet, no place in particular to go . . . or so the boy thought.

They crossed through Osage country without encountering any hostile Indians. They saw a few—and probably a lot more saw them than they realized—but those the father and son spotted were always at a distance, or were not interested in the pair.

"They may be huntin'," Emmett said. "I hear tell Indians is notional folks. Hard for a white man to understand their way of life. I'm told the same band that might leave us alone today, might try to kill us tomorrow."

"Why, Pa?"

"Damned if I know, boy."

"You cussin' again."

"I'm older."

When they reached the Arkansas River, later on that afternoon, Emmett pulled them up and made camp early.

"We got ample powder and shot and paper cartridges, boy. I figure more'n we'll need to get through. According to them I talked with, from here on, it gets mean."

"How's that, Pa?"

"We're headin' west and north as we go. Like this," he drew a line in the dirt with a stick. "This'll take us, I hope, right between the Kiowa and the Pawnee. The white man's been pushin' the Indian hard the past few years, takin' land the Indians say belongs to them. The savages is gettin' right ugly about it, so I'm told."

"Who does the land belong to, Pa?"

Emmett shook his head. "Don't rightly know. Looks to me like it don't *really* belong to nobody. Way I look at it—and most other white folks—a man's gotta *do* something with the land to make it his. The Indians ain't been doing that. So I'm told. They just roam it, hunt it, fish, and the like."

"But how long have they been doing that, Pa?"

The man sighed. He looked at his son. "I 'spect forever, boy."

They rode westward, edging north. Several weeks had passed since they rode from the land of Kirby's birth, and already that place was fading from his mind. He had never been happy there, so he made no real attempt to halt the fading of the images.

Kirby did not know how much his Pa had gotten for the land and the equipment and the mules, but he knew he had gotten it in gold—and not much gold. His Pa carried the gold in a small leather pouch inside his shirt, secured around his neck with a piece of rawhide.

The elder Kirby was heavily armed: a Sharps .52 caliber rifle in a saddle boot, two Remington army revolvers in holsters around his waist, two more pistols in saddle holsters, left and right of the horn. And he carried a gambler's gun behind his belt buckle: a .44 caliber, two-shot derringer. His knife was a wicked-looking, razor-sharp Arkansas Toothpick in a leather sheath on his left side.

Kirby never asked why his father was so heavily armed. But he did ask, "How come them holsters around your waist ain't got no flaps on them, Pa? How come you cut them off that way?"

"So I can get the pistols out faster, son. This leather thong run through the front loops over the hammer to hold the pistol."

"Is gettin' a gun out fast important, Pa?" He knew it was from reading dime novels. But he just could not envision his father as a gunfighter.

"Sometimes, boy. But more important is hittin' what you're aimin' at."

"Think I'll do mine thataway."

"Your choice," the father replied.

Kirby knew, from hearing talk after Appomattox, the Gray was supposed to turn in their weapons. But he had a hunch that his father, hearing of the surrender, had just wheeled around and took the long way back to Missouri, his weapons with him, and the devil with surrender terms.

His dad coughed and asked, "How'd you get that Navy Colt, son?"

"Bunch of Jayhawkers came ridin' through one night, headin' back to Kansas like the devil was chasin' them. Turned out that was just about right. 'Bout a half hour later, Bloody Bill Anderson and his boys came ridin' up. They stopped to rest and water their horses. There was this young feller with them. Couldn't have been no more than a year or so older than me. He seen me and Ma there alone, and all I had was this old rifle." He patted the worn stock of an old flint and percussion Plains' rifle in a saddle boot. "So he give me this Navy gun and an extra cylinder. Seemed like a right nice thing for him to do. He *was* nice, soft-spoken, too."

"It was a nice thing to do. You seen him since?"

"No, sir."

"You thank him proper?"

"Yes, sir. Gave him a bit of food in a sack."

"Neighborly. He tell you his name?"

"Yes, sir. James. Jesse James. His brother Frank was with the bunch, too. Some older than Jesse."

"Don't recall hearin' that name before."

"Jesse blinked his eyes a lot."

"Is that right? Well, you 'member the name, son; might run into him again some day. Good man like that's hard to find."

As the days rolled past, the way ever westward, father and son learned more of the wild country into which they rode, ever alert for trouble, and they learned more of each other. Becoming reacquainted.

They saw herds of buffalo that held them spellbound, the size and number and royal bearing of the magnificent animals awe-inspiring. Even though the animals themselves were stupid. And many times, as they rode, father and son came upon the bones of what appeared to be thousands of the animals, callously slaughtered for their hide, hump, and tongue, the rest left to rot and stink under the summer sun.

"Them is the Indians' main food supply," Emmett told his son. "And another reason why the savages is mad at the whites. I got to side with the savages 'bout this."

As they skirted the rotten bone yard, coyotes and a

few wolves feasted on the tons of meat left behind, Kirby said, "This don't seem right to me."

"Ain't!" Emmett said, his jaw tight with anger. "Man shouldn't never take no more than he hisself can use. This is just pure ol' waste. Stupid."

"And the Indians had nothing to do with this?"

"Hell, no! Look at them shod pony tracks. Indians don't shoe their ponies and drive wagons that left them tracks over there. The white man did this."

They passed the slaughter, both silent for a time. Finally the boy said, "Maybe the Indians have a point about the white man comin' here."

His father spat a brown stream of tobacco juice from the ever present chew tucked in his cheek. "Reckon they do, boy. Not much is ever just black and white . . . always a middle ground that needs lookin' at."

"Like the War between the States, Pa?"

"Yeah. Right and wrong on both sides there, too."

"Was you a hero, Pa?"

"We all was. Ever' man that fought on either side. It was a hell of a war."

"Was you an officer?"

"Sergeant."

"Why was everybody a hero, Pa?"

"'Cause they'll never be—I pray God—another war like that one, boy. Don't know the final count of dead, but it was terrible, I can tell you that."

They plodded on for another mile before the father again spoke. "I seen men layin' side by side, some on stretchers, some on blankets, some just layin' on the cold ground—all of them wounded, lot of them dyin'. The line was five or six deep and it stretched for more'n three miles along the railroad track. You just can't imagine that, boy . . . not until you see it with your own eyes. Maybe one doctor for ever' five hundred men. No medicine, no food, no nothing. Men cryin' out for just the touch of a woman's hand before they died. Toward the end of the war there wasn't even no hope. We knew we was beat, but still we fought on like crazy men."

"Why, Pa?"

"Ask a hundred men, boy, and they'd give you a hundred different answers. They was some men that fought 'cause they really hated the nigras. Some fought 'cause they was losin' a way of life that was all they'd ever known. Some didn't fight at all till they seen the Yankees come through burnin' and lootin' and robbin' and rapin'. And some of them did that, too, boy, don't never let nobody ever tell you no different."

Kirby got a funny feeling in the area just below his belly at the thought of rapin'. He shifted in the saddle.

"I ain't sayin' the Gray didn't have its share of scallywags and white trash, 'cause we did. But nothing to compare with the Yankees."

"Maybe that had something to do with the fact that the Blues had more men, Pa."

Emmett looked at his boy, thinking: *boy's got some smarts about him.* "Maybe so, son."

They rode on, across the seemingly endless plains of tall grass and sudden breaks in the earth, cleverly disguised by nature. A pile of rocks, not arranged by nature, came into view. Kirby pointed them out.

They pulled up. "That's what I been lookin' for," Emmett said. "That's a sign tellin' travelers that this here is the Santa Fe trail. North and west of here'll be Fort Larned. North of that'll be the Pawnee Rock."

"What's that, Pa?"

"A landmark, pilgrim," the voice came from behind the man and his son.

Before Kirby could blink, his pa had wheeled his roan and had a pistol in his hand, hammer back. It was the fastest draw Kirby had ever seen—not that he had seen that many. Just the time the town marshal back in Missouri had tried a fast draw and shot himself in the foot.

"Whoa!" the man said. "You some swift, pilgrim."

"I ain't no pilgrim," Emmett said, low menace in his tone.

Kirby looked at his father; looked at a very new side of the man.

"Reckon you ain't, at that."

Kirby had wheeled his bay and now sat his saddle, staring at the dirtiest man he had ever seen. The man was dressed entirely in buckskin, from the moccasins on his feet to his wide-brimmed leather hat. A white, tobacco-stained beard covered his face. His nose was red and his eyes twinkled with mischief. He looked like a skinny, dirty version of Santa Claus. He sat on a funny-spotted pony, two pack animals with him.

"Where'd you come from?" Emmett asked.

"Been watchin' you two pilgrims from that ravine yonder," he said with a jerk of his head. "Ya'll don't know much 'bout travelin' in Injun country, do you? Best to stay off the ridges. You two been standin' out like a third titty."

He shifted his gaze to Kirby. "What are you starin' at, boy?"

The boy leaned forward in his saddle. "Be durned if I rightly know," he said. And as usual, his reply was an honest one.

The old man laughed. "You got sand to your bottom, all right." He looked at Emmett. "He yourn?"

"My son."

"I'll trade for him," he said, the old eyes sparkling. "Injuns pay right smart for a strong boy like him."

"My son is not for trade, old-timer."

"Tell you what. I won't call you pilgrim, you don't call me old-timer. Deal?"

Emmett lowered his pistol, returning it to leather. "Deal."

"You pil . . . folk know where you are?"

"West of the state of Missouri, east of the Pacific Ocean."

"In other words, you lost as a lizard."

Emmett sighed, more a painful wheezing. "Back south of us is a tradin' post and a few cabins some folks begun callin' Wichita. You heard me say where Fort Larned was."

"Maybe you ain't lost. You two got names?"

"I'm Emmett, this is my son, Kirby."

"Pleasure. I'm called Preacher."

Kirby laughed out loud.

"Don't scoff, boy. It ain't nice to scoff at a man's name. Ifn I wasn't a gentle-type man, I might let the hairs on my neck get stiff."

Kirby grinned. "Preacher can't be your real name."

The old man returned the grin. "Well, no, you right. But I been called that for so long, I nearabouts forgot my Christian name. So, Preacher it'll be. That or nothin'."

"You the one left all them dead buffalo we seen a ways back?" Kirby asked.

"I might have shot one or two. Maybe so, maybe not."

"Seems like a waste to me."

"Did me, too."

"That mean you ain't gonna kill no more?"

"Didn't say that, now, did I?"

Emmett waved Kirby still. "We'll be ridin' on, now, Preacher. Maybe we'll see you again."

Preacher's eyes had shifted to the northwest, then narrowed, his lips tightening. "Yep," he said smiling. "I reckon you will."

Emmett wheeled his horse and pointed its nose west-northwest. Kirby reluctantly followed. He would have liked to stay and talk with the old man.

When they were out of earshot, Kirby said, "Pa, that old man was so dirty he *smelled.*"

"Mountain man. He's a ways from home base, I'm figuring. Tryin' to get back. Cantankerous old boys. Some of them mean as snakes. I think they get together once a year and bathe."

"But you said you soldiered with some mountain men."

"Did. But they got out in time. 'Fore the high lonesome got to them."

"I don't understand."

"They stay up in the high country for years. Don't do nothin' but trap and such. Maybe they won't see a white man once ever' two years—except maybe another mountain man. Sometimes when they do meet, they don't speak. All they've got is their hosses and guns and the whistlin' wind and the silence of the mountains. They're alone. It does something to them. They get notional . . . funny-actin'."

"You mean they go crazy?"

"In a way, I'm thinkin'. I don't know much about them—nobody does, I reckon. But I think maybe they didn't much like people to begin with. They crave the lonesomeness of space. The mountain men I was with, now, they were some different. They told me 'bout that old man's kind. They're brave men, son, don't never doubt that—probably the bravest men in the world. Got to be to live like they do. And what they've done will . . ." He thought for a moment. ". . . con*tri*bute to this country now that we fought the war and can put the nation back together."

"That's a real pretty speech, Pa."

Emmett reddened around the neck.

"What's con*tri*bute?"

"Means they done good."

Kirby looked behind them. "Pa?"

"Son."

"That old man is following us, and he's shucked his rifle out of his boot."

TWO

Preacher galloped up to the pair, his rifle in his hand. "Don't get nervous," he told them. "It ain't me you got to fear. We fixin' to get ambushed . . . shortly. This here country is famous for that."

"Ambushed by who?" Emmett asked, not trusting the old man.

"Kiowa, I think. But they could be Pawnee. My eyes ain't as sharp as they used to be. I seen one of 'em stick a head up out of a wash over yonder, while I was jawin' with you. He's young, or he wouldn't have done that. But that don't mean the others with him is young."

"How many?"

"Don't know. In this country, one's too many. Do know this: We better light a shuck out of here. If memory serves me correct, right over yonder, over that ridge, they's a little crick behind a stand of cottonwoods, old buffalo wallow in front of it." He looked up, stood up in his stirrups, and cocked his shaggy head. "Here they come, boys . . . rake them cayuses!"

Before Kirby could ask what a cayuse was, or what

good a rake was in an Indian attack, the old man had slapped his bay on the rump and they were galloping off. With the mountain man taking the lead, the three of them rode for the crest of the ridge. The pack horses seemed to sense the urgency, for they followed with no pullback on the ropes. Cresting the ridge, the riders slid down the incline and galloped into the timber, down into the wallow. The whoops and cries of the Indians close behind them.

The Preacher might well have been past his so-called good years, but the mountain man had leaped off his spotted pony, rifle in hand, and was in position and firing before Emmett or Kirby had dismounted. Preacher, like Emmett, carried a Sharps .52, firing a paper cartridge, deadly up to seven hundred yards, or more.

Kirby looked up in time to see a brave fly off his pony, a crimson slash on his naked chest. The Indian hit the ground and did not move.

"Get me that Spencer out of the pack, boy," Kirby's father yelled.

"The what?" Kirby had no idea what a Spencer might be.

"The rifle. It's in the pack. A tin box wrapped up with it. Bring both of 'em. Cut the ropes, boy."

Slashing the ropes with his long-bladed knife, Kirby grabbed the long, canvas-wrapped rifle and the tin box. He ran to his father's side. He stood and watched as his father got a buck in the sights of his Sharps, led him on his fast-running pony, then fired. The buck slammed off his pony, bounced off the ground, then leaped to his feet, one arm hanging bloody and broken. The Indian dodged for cover. He didn't make it. Preacher shot him in the side and lifted him off his feet, dropping him dead.

Emmett laid the Sharps aside and hurriedly unwrapped the canvas, exposing an ugly weapon, with a potbellied, slab-sided receiver. Emmett glanced up at Preacher, who was grinning at him.

"What the hell are you grinnin' about, man?"

"Just wanted to see what you had all wrapped up, partner. Figured I had you beat with what's in my pack."

"We'll see," Emmett muttered. He pulled out a thin tube from the tin box and inserted it in the butt plate, chambering a round. In the tin box were a dozen or more tubes, each containing seven rounds, .52 caliber. Emmett leveled the rifle, sighted it, and fired all seven rounds in a thunderous barrage of black smoke. The Indians whooped and yelled. Emmett's firing had not dropped a single brave, but the Indians scattered for cover, disappearing, horses and all, behind a ridge.

"Scared 'em," Preacher opined. "They ain't used to repeaters; all they know is single shots. Let me get something outta my pack. I'll show you a thing or two."

Preacher went to one of his pack animals, untied one of the side packs and let it fall to the ground. He pulled out the most beautiful rifle Kirby had ever seen.

"Damn!" Emmett softly swore. "The blue-bellies had some of those toward the end of the war. But I never could get my hands on one."

Preacher smiled and pulled another Henry repeating rifle from his pack. Unpredictable as mountain men were, he tossed the second Henry to Emmett, along with a sack of cartridges.

"Now we be friends," Preacher said. He laughed,

exposing tobacco-stained stubs of teeth.

"I'll pay you for this," Emmett said, running his hands over the sleek barrel.

"Ain't necessary," Preacher replied. "I won both of 'em in a contest outside Westport Landing. Kansas City to you. 'Sides, somebody's got to look out for the two of you. Ya'll liable to wander 'round out here and get hurt. 'Pears to me don't neither of you know tit from tat 'bout stayin' alive in Injun country."

"You may be right," Emmett admitted. He loaded the Henry. "So thank you kindly."

Preacher looked at Kirby. "Boy, you heeled—so you gonna get in this fight, or not?"

"Sir?"

"Heeled. Means you carryin' a gun, so that makes you a man. Ain't you got no rifle 'cept that muzzle loader?"

"No, sir."

"Take your daddy's Sharps, then. You seen him load it, you know how. Take that tin box of tubes, too. You watch out for our backs. Them Pawnees—and they is Pawnees—likely to come 'crost that crick. You in wild country boy . . . you may as well get bloodied."

"Do it, Kirby," his father said. "And watch yourself. Don't hesitate a second to shoot. Those savages won't show you any mercy, so you do the same to them."

Kirby, a little pale around the mouth, took up the heavy Sharps and the box of tubes, reloaded the rifle, and made himself as comfortable as possible on the rear slope of the slight incline, overlooking the creek.

"Not there, boy." Preacher corrected Kirby's position. "Your back is open to the front line of fire. Get behind that tree 'twixt us and you. That way, you won't catch no lead or arrow in the back."

The boy did as he was told, feeling a bit foolish that he had not thought about his back. Hadn't he read enough dime novels to know that? he chastised himself. Nervous sweat dripped from his forehead as he waited.

He had to go to the bathroom something awful.

A half hour passed, the only action the always moving Kansas winds chasing tumbleweeds, the southward moving waters of the creek, and an occasional slap of a fish.

"What are they waiting for?" Emmett asked the question without taking his eyes from the ridge.

"For us to get careless," Preacher said. "Don't you fret none . . . they still out there. I been livin' in and 'round Injuns the better part of fifty year. I know 'em better—or at least as good—as any livin' white man. They'll try to wait us out. They got nothing but time, boys."

"No way we can talk to them?" Emmett asked, and immediately regretted saying it as Preacher laughed.

"Why, shore, Emmett," the mountain man said. "You just stand up, put your hands in the air, and tell 'em you want to palaver some. They'll probably let you walk right up to 'em. Odds are, they'll even let you speak your piece; they polite like that. A white man can ride right into nearabouts any Injun village. They'll feed you, sign-talk to you, and give you a place a sleep. Course . . . gettin' *out* is the problem.

"They ain't like us, Emmett. They don't come close to thinkin' like us. What is fun to them is torture to us. They call it testin' a man's bravery. Ifn a man dies good—that is, don't holler a lot—they make it last as long as possible. Then they'll sing songs about you, praise you for dyin' good. Lots of white folks condemn 'em for that, but it's just they way of life.

"They got all sorts of ways to test a man's bravery and strength. They might—dependin' on the tribe—strip you, stake you out over a big anthill, then pour honey over you. Then they'll squat back and watch, see how well you die."

Kirby felt sick at his stomach.

"Or they might bury you up to your neck in the ground, slit your eyelids so you can't close 'em, and let the sun blind you. Then, after your eyes is burnt blind, they'll dig you up and turn you loose naked out in the wild . . . trail you for days, seein' how well you die."

Kirby positioned himself better behind the tree and quietly went to the bathroom. If a bean is a bean, the boy thought, what's a pea? A relief.

Preacher just wouldn't shut up about it. "Out in the deserts, now, them Injuns get downright mean with they fun. They'll cut out your eyes, cut off your privates, then slit the tendons in your ankles so's you can't do nothin' but flop around on the sand. They get a big laugh out of that. Or they might hang you upside down over a little fire. The 'Paches like to see hair burn. They a little strange 'bout that.

"Or, if they like you, they might put you through what they call the run of the arrow. I lived through that . . . once. But I was some younger. Damned ifn I want to do it agin at my age. Want me to tell you 'bout that little game?"

"No!" Emmett said quickly. "I get your point."

"Figured you would. Point is, don't let 'em ever take you alive. Kirby, now, they'd probably keep for work or trade. But that's chancy, he being nearabout a man growed." The mountain man tensed a bit, then said, "Look alive, boy, and stay that way. Here they come." He winked at Kirby.

"How do you know that, Preacher?" Kirby asked. "I don't see anything."

"Wind just shifted. Smelled 'em. They close, been easin' up through the grass. Get ready."

Kirby wondered how the old man could smell anything over the fumes from his own body.

Emmett, a veteran of four years of continuous war, could not believe an enemy could slip up on him in open daylight. At the sound of Preacher jacking back the hammer of his Henry .44, Emmett shifted his eyes from his perimeter for just a second. When he again looked back at his field of fire, a big, painted-up buck was almost on top of him. Then the open meadow was filled with screaming, charging Indians.

Emmett brought the buck down with a .44 slug through the chest, flinging the Indian backward, the yelling abruptly cut off in his throat.

The air had changed from the peacefulness of summer quiet to a screaming, gunsmoke-filled hell. Preacher looked at Kirby, who was looking at him, his mouth hanging open in shock, fear, and confusion. "Don't look at me, boy!" he yelled. "Keep them eyes in front of you."

Kirby jerked his gaze to the small creek and the stand of timber that lay behind it. His eyes were beginning to smart from the acrid powder smoke, and his head was aching from the pounding of the Henry .44 and the screaming and yelling. The Spencer Kirby held at the ready was a heavy weapon, and his arms were beginning to ache from the strain.

His head suddenly came up, eyes alert. He had seen movement on the far side of the creek. Right there! Yes, someone, or something was over there.

I don't want to shoot anyone, the boy thought. *Why can't we be friends with these people?* And that thought was still throbbing in his brain when a young Indian suddenly sprang from the willows by the creek and lunged into the water, a rifle in his hand.

For what seemed like an eternity, Kirby watched the young brave, a boy about his own age, leap and thrash through the water. Kirby jacked back the hammer of the Spencer, sighted in the brave, and pulled the trigger. The .52 caliber pounded his shoulder, bruising it, for there wasn't much spare meat on Kirby. When the smoke blew away, the young Indian was face down in the water, his blood staining the stream.

Kirby stared at what he'd done, then fought back waves of sickness that threatened to spill from his stomach.

The boy heard a wild screaming and spun around. His father was locked in hand-to-hand combat with two knife-wielding braves. Too close for the rifle, Kirby clawed his Navy Colt from leather, vowing he would cut that stupid flap from his holster after this was over. He shot one brave through the head just as his father buried his Arkansas Toothpick to the hilt in the chest of the other.

And as abruptly as they came, the Indians were gone, dragging as many of their dead and wounded with them as they could. Two braves lay dead in front of Preacher; two braves lay dead in the shallow ravine with the three men; the boy Kirby had shot lay in the creek, arms outstretched, the waters a deep crimson.

The body slowly floated downstream.

Preacher looked at the dead buck in the creek, then at the brave in the wallow with them . . . the one Kirby had shot. He lifted his eyes to the boy.

"Got your baptism this day, boy. Did right well, you did."

"Saved my life, son," Emmett said, dumping the bodies of the Indians out of the wallow. "Can't call you boy no more, I reckon. You be a man, now."

A thin finger of smoke lifted from the barrel of the Navy .36 Kirby held in his hand. Preacher smiled and spat tobacco juice.

He looked at Kirby's ash-blond hair. "Yep," he said. "Smoke'll suit you just fine. So Smoke hit'll be."

"Sir?" Kirby finally found his voice.

"Smoke. That's what I'll call you now on. Smoke."

THREE

Preacher hopped out of the wallow and walked to a dead buck. He bent down and removed something from the dead Indian's belt. A Navy .36. He tossed the pistol to Kirby, along with a sack of shot and powder.

"Here, Smoke. Now you got two of 'em."

Kirby felt more than a little foolish with his new nickname. He did not feel at all like a man called Smoke should feel. Tough and brave and gallant and all that. But he smiled, secretly liking his new name.

Off another dead Indian, Preacher took a long-bladed knife, in a bead-adorned sheath. He tossed that to Kirby. "Man's gotta have a good knife, too."

Then he pulled his own knife and began scalping the dead bucks.

"Good God, man!" Emmett protested. "What in the hell are you doing?"

"Takin' hair," Preacher said. "I know a tradin' post that pays a dollar for ever' scalp lock a man can bring in. Fifty cents for a squaw's hair. But I don't hold with scalpin' wimmin. I won't do this to a Ute or a Crow—

lived with 'em too long, I reckon—but I just purely can't abide a Pawnee."

Emmett grimaced at the bloody sight but kept his mouth shut. He had heard that Indians had not been the originators of scalping, but the white man. Now he believed the story.

Kirby looked on as Preacher took the Indian's hair. He was both horrified and fascinated.

Neither Emmett nor his son had ever seen a warlike Indian. There had been a few down-at-the-heels Quapaw Indians in Missouri when Emmett was growing up—and were still a few around—but they were not warlike. Father and son moved closer to take a look at their recent enemy.

Preacher had finished his grisly work. Surprisingly, to Kirby, at least, there was little blood from the close haircut.

"They don't look so mean to me . . . not now, anyways," Kirby said. "They just look . . . kinda poor."

"They ain't poor," Preacher contradicted. "Don't you believe that for a second. Most of the time they eat right well. Buffalo steak's nearabouts the best meat in the world, I reckon. And pemmican." He rolled his eyes and Kirby laughed at the old man's antics. "Well, you ever get a chance to eat some pemmican, you see what I mean. Tasty. Indian goes hungry, it's his own fault. They won't grow no gardens. They think that's beneath 'em. Warriors and hunters, not farmers. So to hell with 'em."

"Do you grow a garden, Preacher?" Kirby asked.

"I been known to from time to time. But I ain't no gawddamned sodbuster, if that's what you mean."

"See, Pa." Kirby looked at his father. "He can cuss. Why can't I?"

"Hush up, Kirby."

"What's that about cussin'?" Preacher asked.

"Never mind," Emmett said.

Kirby was growing accustomed to the dead braves. They did not bother him now. His stomach had ceased its growling. "What'd you call that food? Pem . . . what?"

"Buffalo meat, usually. Indians cut it into strips, dry it. That's called jerky. They take the jerky, crumble it, then beat hell out of it. Then they mix it with fleece—"

"With what?"

"Fat. Boilin' fat. Then you drop in a few berries, make it up in a brick, and wrap it. Best eatin' you ever put in your mouth. Don't spoil. Lasts for months. Shore do." He put his bloody scalps into a pouch on his wide belt and closed the flap.

"Won't those stink?" Kirby asked.

"They do get right ripe," the mountain man admitted.

"Do we bury these Indians?" Emmett inquired.

"Hell no!" Preacher looked horrified. "Plains' Injuns don't plant they dead like we do. 'Sides, they be back for 'em, don't you fret about that. Right now, I 'spect we better git from here. Put some country 'twixt us and them live Injuns. Let's go."

The trio rode at a steady gallop for several miles, then walked their horses, resting them as best they could. They repeated this several times, putting miles between them and the battle site by the creek. Late afternoon, they pulled up by a tiny stream and made a short camp.

"We'll make the fire small," Preacher said. "Use them dry buffalo chips we picked up. They don't hardly make no smoke. We'll have us coffee and beans, then douse the fire and make camp 'bout two-three miles from here. Place I 'member. We'll post guards this night, boys, and ever' night from here on in." He glanced at Kirby. "This is hostile country, Smoke."

Kirby sighed. He guessed it was going to be Smoke for the rest of his life. Or at least until Preacher left them. He looked at his Pa. Emmett was smiling.

Kirby said nothing until the fire was glowing faintly and the coffee boiling. The beans cooked, he sliced bacon into a blackened skillet then looked at Preacher.

"Why Smoke, Preacher?"

"All famous men got to have good-soundin' nick-names—impressive ones. Smoke sounds good to me. And believe me, Smoke, I have known some right famous men in my time."

"I'm not famous," Kirby said, a confused look on his face. Already a nice-looking boy, he would be a handsome man.

"You will be, I'm thinkin'," the mountain man said stretching out on the ground. "You will be." And he would say no more about it.

They ate an early supper, then doused the fire, carefully checking for any live coals that might touch off a prairie fire, something as feared as any Indian attack, for a racing fire could outrun a galloping horse. They moved on, riding for an hour before pulling into a small stand of timber to make camp. Preacher spread his blankets, used his saddle for a pillow, and promptly closed his eyes.

Emmett said, "I'll stand the first watch . . . Smoke," and he grinned. "Then wake Preacher for the second, and you can take the last watch, from two till daylight. Best you go on to sleep now, you'll need it."

Just as Kirby was drifting off to sleep, Emmett said, "If you don't like that nickname, son, we can change it."

"It's all right, Pa," the boy murmured, warmed by the wool of the blanket. "Pa? I kinda like Preacher."

"So do I, son."

"That makes both of you good judges of character," the mountain man spoke from his blankets. "Now why don't you two quit all that jawin' and let an old man get some rest?"

"Night, Pa—Preacher."

"Night, Smoke," they both replied.

Preacher rolled the boy out of his blankets at two in the morning, into the summer coolness on the Plains. The night was hung with the brilliance of a million stars.

"Stay sharp, now, Smoke," Preacher cautioned. "Injun don't usually attack at night; bad medicine for them. Brave gets kilt at night, his spirit wanders forever, don't never get to the Hereafter in peace. But Injuns is notional, and not all tribes believe the same. Never can tell what they're gonna do. More'un likely, if they're out there, they'll hit us at first light—but you don't never know for shore." He rolled into his blankets and was soon snoring.

The boy poured a tin cup full of scalding, hot coffee, strong enough to support a horseshoe, then replaced the pot on the rock grate. Preacher had showed him how to build the fire, surrounded by rocks, larger rocks in the center to support a pan or pot, the fire hot, but no bigger than a hand. The air opening lay at the rear, facing the camp. The fire was fueled by buffalo chips, hot and smokeless, and the fire could not be seen from ten feet away.

While there was still light, Kirby (he could not bring himself to even think of himself as Smoke) had carefully cleaned and oiled the Navy Colt taken from the dead Indian. He had cut the flap off his holster and punched a hole in the front of the leather, threading a piece of rawhide through the hole, the loop to be placed over the hammer, securing the weapon. He did the same to a holster Preacher gave him, for his second weapon, then, using a wide belt—also given him by Preacher, from his seemingly never emptying packs—he buckled on his twin .36s. The right hand pistol he wore butt back, the left hand pistol, he carried butt forward, slightly higher than the other pistol. The big-bladed bowie knife was in its bead-adorned sheath, just behind the left hand Colt.

He hàd no way of knowing at this juncture of his young life, but with that action involving the pistols, and with what would follow in only a matter of hours, he was taking the first steps toward creating a legend that would endure as long as writers would write of the West. Men would fear and respect him; women would desire him but only one would ever find herself truly loved by him; children would play games, imitating the man called Smoke, and songs would be written and sung about him, both in the Indian villages and in the white man's saloons.

But on this pleasant night, Kirby was still some years away from being a living legend: He was just a slightly frightened young man, just a few months into his sixteenth year, sitting in the middle of a vast open plain, watching for savage Indians and hoping to God none were within a thousand miles of him. He almost dozed off, caught himself, and jerked back awake. He bent forward to pour another cup of coffee, rubbing his sleepy eyes as he did so.

That movement saved his life.

A quivering arrow drove into the tree where Kirby, just a second before, had been resting. Had he not leaned forward, the arrow would have driven through his chest.

Although Kirby had not yet practiced his gun moves, he had carefully gone over them in his mind. He drew first the right hand Colt, then the left hand gun, the heavy bark of one only a split second behind the first. Always a well-coordinated boy, his motions were almost liquid in their smoothness, the Colts in the hands of one of those few to whom guns seem almost an extension of the body. Two Pawnee braves went down in lifeless heaps. Kirby shifted position and the Navy Colts blasted the night in thunderous roars. Two more bucks were cut down by the .36 caliber balls.

Then the smoke-filled night was silent except for the fading sounds of Indian ponies racing away, away from the white man's camp. The Indians wanted no more of this camp: They had lost too many braves; too much death here.

"I ain't never seen nothin' like this!" Preacher exclaimed, walking around the dead and dying Pawnee. "I knowed Jim Bridger, Kit Carson, Broken Hand Fitzpatrick, Uncle Dick Wooten, and Rattlesnake Williams . . . and a hundred other salty ol' boys. But I ain't never seen nothin' to top this here. Smoke, you may be a youngster in years, but you'll damn shore do to ride the river with."

Kirby did not yet know it, but that was the highest compliment a mountain man could give another man.

"Thank you," he said to Preacher. He reloaded the empty cylinders.

Preacher scalped the Pawnee, then tossed the bloody scalp locks to Kirby. "They yourn, Smoke. Put 'em in that war bag I give you. They worth four dollars to you. Go on . . . four dollars ain't nothin' to sneeze at."

With his father watching him through eyes that had seen much, Kirby picked up the bloody hair and placed them in a beaded pouch Preacher had given him.

Emmett, who had ridden with the great Confederate Ranger, J. S. Mosby for a year, was the furthest from being a stranger to guns and gunplay. Although Kirby would not learn of it for years, his father had been with Mosby when they rode into the middle of a Union Army camp at Fairfax, Virginia one night. They had asked their way to headquarters and there, Mosby awakened the Yankee general, Stoughton, by rudely and ungentlemanly slapping the man on his butt.

"Have you ever heard of J. S. Mosby," the Confederate guerrilla asked in a whisper.

Angry, the general replied, "Of course! Have you captured him?"

"No," Mosby said with a smile. "He's captured you."

The Confederate Rangers then kidnapped the Union general from under the noses of the general's own men.

"You're smooth and quick," Emmett complimented his son. "And I have seen some men who were smooth and quick."

"Thank you, Pa," Kirby said. He was just a little bit sick and embarrassed by what he'd done and all the attention he was receiving. The scalp locks in his war bag were not helping his stomach any.

"Be careful how you use your newfound talent, son," the father cautioned. "Use it for good, and not for evil. Temper your talent."

Then the man coughed and thought of his own mission westward. He wondered how and when he should tell his son.

"Yes, Pa. I will."

Preacher looked at the boy and wondered.

The trio rode for several days without encountering any more hostiles. They saw smoke, often, and knew they were being watched and discussed, but they rode through without further incident from the Pawnee. Three of them had killed more than twelve Pawnee, wounding several more in two quick fights. The Indian may have been a savage—to the white man's way of reasoning—but he was not a fool, and he was a first-class fighting man, many of the tribes the greatest guerrilla fighters the world would ever know. Part of that is knowing when to fight and when to back off. This was definitely one of the back-off times.

"This here is the Cimarron Cutoff," Preacher said.

They had pulled up and sat their horses, the man and boy looking where he pointed. "The southern route to Santa Fe. Better for wagons and women, but the water is scarce. The northern route is best for water and graze, but it's tough. Lord, it's tough."

"Why?" Emmett asked.

"Mountains. Rocky Mountains. Make them mountains where I's born look like pimples."

"Where is that, Preacher?" Kirby asked.

"East Tennysee. Long time ago." His eyes clouded briefly with memories of a home he had not seen in more than half a century. At first the man had planned to return for a visit, but as the years rolled by, those plans dimmed, never becoming reality. Then he realized his Ma and Pa would be dead—long dead—and there was no point in going back.

The price many men paid for forging westward, opening up new trails for the thousands that would follow.

"I run off when I were twelve," Preacher said, looking at father and son. "That were, best I can recall, fifty-two year ago, 1813, I believe it was. I've spent the better part of fifty year in the mountains. And I reckon I've known ever' mountain man worth his salt in that time, and some that thought they was tough, but weren't."

"What happened to them that wasn't?" Kirby asked.

"I helped bury some of 'em," Preacher said quietly.

"You must know your way around this country, then," Emmett said.

"Do for a fact. I helped open up this here Santa Fe Trail, and I've ridden the Mormon Trail more'un once. Boys, I been up the mountain, over the hill, and 'crost the river. And I've seen the varmit." He looked hard at Kirby. "But Smoke, I swear I ain't never seen the likes of you when it comes to handlin' a short gun. It's like you was born with a Colt in your hands. Unnatural."

The old mountain man was silent for a time, his eyes on the deep ruts in the ground that signified the Santa Fe Trail. "I don't know where you two is goin'. Probably you don't neither. You may be just a-wanderin', that's all. Lookin'. That's dandy. Good for folk to see the country. So I'll tag along here and there, catch up ever' now and then see how you're a-makin' it. I usually don't much take to folk. Like to be alone. Must be a sign of my *ad*-vanced age, my kinda takin' a likin' to you two. 'Specially Smoke, there. I got a feelin' 'bout him. He's gonna make a name for hisself. I want to see that; be there when he do."

"We're heading, in a roundabout way," Emmett said, "to a place called I-dee-ho."

"Rugged and beautiful," Preacher said. "Been there lots of times. But were I you—'course I ain't—I'd see Colorado first. Tell you what: I got me a cache of fur not too far from here. Last year's trappin'. Ya'll mosey around, take it easy, and keep on headin' northwest. From here, more north than west. Ya'll will cut the northern trail of the Santa Fe in a few days. Stay with it till you come to the ruins of Bent's Fort. I'll meet you there. See you." He wheeled his horses and rode off without looking back, pack horses in tow.

Emmett looked at his son. Preacher liked the boy. And if he would agree to see to him through the waning months of his boyhood . . . well, Emmett's mission could wait. The men he hunted would still be there. But for now, he wanted to spend some time with his son.

"How about it, Kirby—I mean, Smoke. Want to see Colorado?"

The boy-rapidly-turning-man grinned. "Sure, Pa."

Long before 1865, Bent's Fort lay in ruins. But from 1834 to 1850, the post ruled the fur trade in the southern Rockies. By 1865, the mountain men were almost no more. Time had caught up with them, and in most cases, passed them by. Civilization had raised its sometimes dubious head and pushed the mountain men into history. Those that remained were men, for the most part, advanced in years (for their time), heading for the sunset of their lives. But they were still a rough breed, tough and salty, not to be taken lightly or talked down to. For these men had spent their youth, their best years, and the midpoint of their lives, in the elements, where one careless move could have meant either sudden death or slow torture from hostiles. Mountain men were not easily impressed.

But the gathering of mountain men stood and watched as Kirby and his father rode slowly into the ruins of the old post, rifles across their saddles, pack animals trailing.

Kirby and his father did not know Preacher had spread the word about the boy called Smoke.

Kirby, as did many boys of that hard era, looked older than his years. His face was deeply tanned, and he was rawboned, just beginning to fill out for his adult life. His shoulders and arms were lean, but hard with muscle, and they would grow much harder and powerful in the months ahead.

"He don't look like much to me," an aging mountain man said to a friend.

"Neither did Kit," his friend replied. "Warn't but four inches over five feet. But he were a hell of a man."

The mountain man nodded. "That he were." His eyes were on Kirby. "Funny way to wear a brace of short guns."

"Faster than a snake, Preacher says."

The mountain man cocked an eye at his friend. "Preacher's been known to tell a lie ever' now and then."

"Not this time, I wager. That there kid's got a mean look to his eyes. Mayhaps he don't know it yet, but he do. Give him two-three years, I'd think long 'fore tanglin' with him."

That got him an astonished look. "Hell-fire, Calico. You fit a grizzly once!"

"Won, too," the old man said. "But I'm thinkin' that kid's part bear, part puma, part rattler. I'll go 'long with Preacher on this one."

"Does have a certain set to that squared-off jaw, don't he?"

"Yep. Big hands on him."

Kirby and Emmett sat their horses and stared. Neither had ever seen anything like this colorful assemblage. The men (only a few squaws were in attendance and they stayed to themselves), all of them sixty-plus in years, were dressed in wild, bright colors: in buckskin breeches and shirt, with beaded leggings, wide red or blue or yellow sashes about their waists. Some wore whipcord trousers, with silk shirts shining in a cacophony of colors. All were beaded and booted and bearded. Some held long muzzle-loading Kentucky rifles, or Plains' rifles, with colorfully dyed rawhide dangling from the barrel, the shot and powder bags decorated with beads.

This was to be the last great gathering of the magnificent breed of men called Mountain Man. Many of them, after this final rendezvous in the twilight of their years, would drift back into the great mountains they loved, never to be heard from or seen again, to die as they had lived—alone. Their graves the earth they explored, their monuments the mountains they loved, tombstones rearing above them forever. They were a breed of man that flourished but briefly, whose courage and light helped to open the way west.

When Emmett and Kirby spotted Preacher, they could not believe their eyes. They sat their horses and stared.

Preacher was clean, his beard trimmed. He wore new buckskins, new leggings, a red sash around his waist, and a light they had never seen sparkled from his eyes. "Howdy!" he called. "Ya'll light and sit, boys."

"I don't believe it," Emmett said. "His face is clean."

"Water to wash in over there," Preacher said, pointing. "Good strong soap, too. But you'd best dump what's in the barrel, though. It's got fleas in with the ticks."

When Emmett and son walked out into the final rendezvous of the mountain men, on this, their first day at the old post, they were greeted warmly, if with a bit of constraint.

"Gonna have us a feast," a one-eyed, grizzled old

man told them. "Come on. Got buffalo hump, antelope, and puma. Preacher's gonna give up the message. Let's don't be late."

"Puma?" Kirby questioned.

"Mountain lion," the man told him. "Best, sweetest meat you ever did taste." He smacked his lips. "This is the first big rendezvous I've been to in more'un twenty year. Guess this will be the last one for many of us," he added, sadness in his voice.

"Why?" Kirby asked.

"Fur trade's damn near gone; pilgrims pourin' in over the trails me and all the others opened up. Hate to see it. Why, I seen five white people just last month. Five! Gettin' so's a body can't even be alone no more."

"When was your last rendezvous?" Emmett asked. Even he had never seen anything to compare with this gathering.

The mountain man stopped and scratched his head. "Let me ponder on that. Oh, back 'bout '40, I reckon."

"But this is 1865!" Kirby said.

"It is! Well, damn me. Time shore do get away from a body, don't it?"

"They'll be many more people behind us," Emmett said.

"Yep. I reckon there will be. Be a plumb ruination to the country, too." He shook his head and walked away to join a small group of aging mountain men gathered around several smoking pits just outside of what was left of the fort.

The fort, built in a sheltered bend of the Arkansas River, had been for years a welcome sight to trappers, traders, and the few travelers, representing a bit of safe haven for man and horse.

Sad, Kirby thought, his eyes taking in all the sights and sounds and good smells of cooking. It's sad. These men opened up this country, and now they're old, and nobody wants them around.

And that just did not seem right nor fair to the tall young man.

As if on silent cue, the men gathered in a circle. Preacher walked to the center of the circle, and the babble of voices fell silent.

"Well, boys," he said in a somber voice. "I reckon this here rendezvous is 'bout gonna do it for most of us. Our time is past. We got to move over, make way for civilized folk: ranches and farms and plows and wire and pilgrims and the like.

"But boys, we can always 'member this: We saw it first and them few that come 'fore us. We seen it when it was glory. Untouched. We rode the mountains and the rivers, we made the trails for the pilgrims to foller, and we buried our friends—when we could find enuff of 'em to bury. Some of us was the first white man an eagle or bear or Injun ever seen. Now it's nearabouts time for some of us to see the elephant. But that's got to be all right. We done, I believe, what we was put on this here earth to do, and we can all be right proud we done it.

"Streams trapped out, purt-near. Fools comin' in a-killin' all the buffalo. In some parts they's stringin' wire all over God's creation. A-hemmin' us in."

He slowly turned, his eyes touching the gaze of all present.

"But where can we go?" Preacher asked.

No one could answer the question.

"We never married nobody 'ceptin' squaws. Got no white kin to go back to. Even if we did, they wouldn't have us. Can you see us livin' in a town? All cooped up like a wild animal? No, sir. Not me. Not for none of you, I'm thinkin'.

"For me, I'm gonna see to it that this here boy, Smoke," he cut his eyes to Kirby, "learns the true way of the wilderness. Might take me awhile, him being no more than a child. But . . . I reckon he's as old as we was when we come out here, green as a gourd and wet behind the ears.

"And when that's done, I'm gonna fork my horses and ride out to see this here much-talked about elephant.

"But, 'fore that happens, we all gonna eat, tell lies to one 'nother, and whoop and holler and dance. Then we just gonna ride out without lookin' back. 'Cause boys, it's all over for men like us, and for some of us, real soonlike, we got just one more trail to ride."

Kirby looked around him, seeing tears in some eyes of the mountain men. For they knew the words they were hearing were true.

Preacher took a deep breath. "Now, boys, bow your blasphemous old heads, 'cause I'm a-gonna talk to the Lord 'fore we feast.

"Oh, Lord," his voice was strong, carrying far beyond the circle of men, "thanks for this grub we 'bout to partake of. We'll enjoy, I'm sure, 'cause them smells is startin' my mouth to salavatin'. But 'fore we start a-gummin' and a-gnawin' on this sweet meat, there's something I got to ask You. Do You ever think You maybe made a mistake in the way You set a man up to go down his final trail? Give it some thought, Lord. Here we are, old men past our prime, juices all dried up. Couldn't do nothin' with a woman 'cept think about it and some of us forgot what it was we could even think of. But we're a-smellin' all the good smells of cookin'. Point I'm makin', Lord, is this: If You ever want to do it again, do this: When a man gets our age, take his balls and give him back his teeth!

"Amen—let's eat."

FOUR

Two days later, when Kirby awakened at dawn and kicked off his blankets, a curious silence surrounded him. A feeling of aloneness. Pulling on pants and boots over his long-handles, he looked around the ruins of the old post. Nothing. The mountain men were gone, having pulled out as silently as they had learned to live. He shook his father awake and told him what had happened.

On his feet, his father pointed. "Over there."

Preacher stood on the banks of the Arkansas, his face to the high mountains.

"What's he doin', Pa?"

"Sayin' goodbye, Kirby. In his own way." He glanced at his son. "That old man likes you, son. Listen to him, and he'll teach you things you'll need to stay alive in this country."

The son met the father's eyes. "I will, Pa."

The father patted the boy's shoulder and then coughed.

* * *

The three of them rode out the next morning. They headed for the tall, shining mountains.

"Where will your friends go, Preacher?" Kirby asked. The day the mountain men had left, Preacher had spent to himself, speaking to no one. But on this day he was his usual garrulous self.

"They'll scatter, Smoke. Most of 'em will head back into the mountains, find 'em a lonely valley, and they'll never come out again. A few still got people back East, and they'll head there. But they won't stay; 'less they die there. It'll be too tame for 'em. And they own people won't want 'em around more'un four-five days. Then they'll want to get shut of 'em."

"That's sad. Why won't they want them?"

"Back East, Smoke, they got written laws a body's got to live by. Ain't none of us followed no law 'cept our own for more'un fifty years. Law of common sense. You don't put hands on 'nother man; don't steal from him; don't cheat him; don't call him a liar. Do, and you gonna get killed. Out here, Smoke, man purty well respects the rights of the other feller, and don't none of us need no gawddamned lawyer to tell us how to do that. It'll be that way out here for a while longer, till the fancy people get all het up and mess it all up. The worse is yet to come, Smoke. You wait and see. Thank Gawd I won't be around to see it. I'd have to puke."

"How do you mean: Mess it all up?"

"Lawyers readin' meanin's into words that ain't 'posed to be there. A-messin' up what should be left up to common sense. Hell's fire, Smoke. Rattlesnake crawls into your blankets with you, you don't ask him ifn he's gonna bite you. You kick him out and shoot him or stomp him. Same with man. Man does you a deliberate wrong—and don't never let no smooth-talkin' lawyer man tell you no different, Smoke, ever'body knows right from wrong—you go after that man; you settle up your way. To hell with lawyers—damn ever'one of 'em."

"I'll go along with you on that, Preacher," Emmett said. "That's one of the reasons I brought my son out here."

"Well . . . Smoke's got maybe twenty-five years 'fore this country gets all worded up with them fancy-pants lawyers. After that, a man won't be able to be a man no more. And it's comin', boys, bet on it."

Preacher looked around him. "Well, ain't no use frettin' 'bout it now. 'Cause right now we got our hair to worry 'bout. We gonna be travelin' through hostile country, and the Sand Crick massacre is still fresh in the minds of the Injuns.

"Soldiers wiped out an entar Injun village: men, wimmin, papooses. Mostly Cheyenne and some Arapaho. Black Kettle was they chief. Happened last year and the Injuns still got hard feelins 'bout that. A Colonel Chivington was in charge, so I'm told."

"Will we pass by it?" Kirby asked.

"No. It's north and some east of here. But I seen it right after it happened. Damn near made me puke. There weren't no call for it. Black Kettle's brother, White Antelope, was killed that raid. And Black Kettle ain't no man to mess with. Left Hand, a chief of the Arapaho, showed his bravery and scorn of the white men by standin' in front of his tent with his arms folded crost his chest, refusin' to fight. Damn soldiers kilt him, too." Preacher spat on the ground.

"White men ain't no saints, Smoke. They can be just

as mean and orne'y as they claim the Injuns to be."

"Where is Black Kettle now?" Emmett asked, his eyes on the huge mountains in front of them.

"On the warpath. So ifn either of you gets to feelin' your hair start to tingle, let me know, 'cause they's Injuns close by."

"I'll be sure to do that," Emmett said dryly.

For the next several days, they followed the Arkansas River, then cut northwest through the Arkansas valley. Kiowa country, Preacher told them. So stay alert. It was here that Kirby's frontier education really began.

"I ain't never seen the likes of this," the boy said, his eyes sweeping the panorama of nature.

"They's lots of things you ain't seen, Smoke," Preacher said. "But you will, I'm figuring. Ifn you don't get mauled by a bear, bit by a rattler, fall off your horse and break your neck, get caught up in a landslide or blizzard, eat bad meat or drink pisen water, shoot yourself in the foot and bleed to death, or get your hair lifted by Injuns."

Kirby swallowed hard. He pointed to plants on the desolate brown hills. "What's them things?"

"Them's prickly pear and ball cactus. In the spring, both have right purty flowers on 'em. Over there," he pointed, "is yucca. Them long tall white flowers on 'em is what the Spanish call Madonna Candles. Named after they momma, I guess, don't rightly know."

Emmett laughed at that and Preacher ignored him.

"You see, Smoke, most ever'thing the good Lord

created can be used for something. The injuns use the guts of them plants to make rope—good stout rope, too. I know; I been tied up with it a time or two. And ifn you feel in need of a bath—and a man ought to get wet with water two-three times a year—you can dig up some yucca root and use it for soap. Makes a good lather. Keep that in mind ifn you start to get real gamy. But don't overdo baths. I believe a body needs a chance to rest."

Emmett laughed and then coughed for a few seconds. His coughing had gotten worse the past week. But he offered no explanation for his cough and neither Preacher nor Kirby asked.

"Up here a ways," Preacher said, "we'll bear a little more west. Head for a tradin' post I know—called Pueblo."

Emmett looked at him. "I've heard that name."

"It's known a bit. 'Count of the Mormons, mostly. Back in . . . oh . . . '46 or '47, Mormons tried to make a settlement there. I come up on 'em time a two. They notional folk, don't believe like we do. Don't never talk religion with 'em—mess up your mind. I try to keep shy of 'em."

"What happened to the people who tried to settle there?" Kirby asked.

"Don't rightly know. I come back through there—me and Rattlesnake Williams—oh . . . I reckon it were '52 or '53, and we didn't see hide nor hair of 'em. I heared tell they went up north, back to Utah. Don't get me wrong; they good folk. Help you out ifn you need a hand. But you best know what you're doin' ifn you plan on tradin' with 'em. They good traders. And don't mess with they wimmin folk. They get real touchy 'bout they females."

The only thing Kirby knew about females was that they were different from men. Just exactly how they were different was still a mystery to him. He had asked his Pa a time or two, but Emmett got all red in the face and cleared his throat a lot. Said he'd tell Kirby when the time came. So far, the time had not yet come.

Kirby remembered the time, three years back, when a carnival came through his part of Missouri. One of the girls, just about his own age, had made a bunch of eyes at him. She'd cornered Kirby at the edge of the lot and told him for two dollars she'd make a man out of him. Then she reached down with her hand and grabbed Kirby. *Nobody* had ever grabbed him there. Scared him so bad he took off into the woods and was running so hard he ran right into a tree. Knocked himself unconscious for half an hour.

Kirby had never told anybody about that.

"Where's Utah?" Kirby asked.

"West of us. You'll see it one of these days, Smoke."

They pulled up to rest and Kirby's bay began tugging at the reins, trying to head off east. Kirby finally had to brutally jerk the reins to settle the animal.

"Smells water," Preacher told him. He pointed to a small water hole. "But that's bad water. Pisen. Horse sometimes ain't got no sense when it comes to water. Injuns call that water wau-nee-chee. Means no good."

Kirby rolled that word around his tongue, memorizing it. "How can you tell if water is no good?"

"Look for bones of small animals and birds closeby. Can't always go by smell or taste." He swung his spotted pony. "You'll learn, Smoke. I'll teach you."

Emmett finally asked the question that had been on

his mind for days. "Why, Preacher?"

"Gettin' old," the mountain man said simply and softly. "Like to leave something of what I know behind when I go see the elephant. Got no one else to leave it with."

"You were never married?"

Preacher laughed. "Hell's fire, yes! Five—no, six times. Injun ceremonies. I got twelve-fifteen younguns runnin' 'round out here. Half-breeds. But most of 'em don't know me for what I am, and I don't know them. That weren't the way I planned it; it just worked out that way. Wouldn't know most of 'em ifn I saw 'em. I'm just 'nother white man. They'd soon shoot me and take my hair as look at me. Probably rather shoot me than look at me, ifn the truth be told."

"Why?" Emmett asked.

"They breeds, that's why. Some tribes don't look with much favor on breeds. Then they's them that being a breed don't make no difference. Injuns ain't all alike, Smoke. They just as different in thinkin' as white men, and just as quarrelsome, too—with other tribes. Ifn the Injun would ever try to git along and unite agin us, the white man would have never got past Kansas. I think Injuns is the greatest fighters the world'll ever know. But they just can't get together agin us. Something I'm right thankful for," he added.

They took their time getting to Pueblo with Kirby learning more from the old mountain man each day. And he was eager to learn, retaining all the old man told him. The weeks on the trail had begun the transformation of the boy into the edge of manhood.

Sixteen, Emmett mused as they rode, and already killed half a dozen men. His son's quickness and ease with the Navy Colts had stuck in the man's mind. The father had handled guns all his life. Before taking up farming, he had been marshal of a small town in Missouri, on the Kansas border, and had killed two men during his tenure in office. God alone knew how many men he had killed in the war. But Kirby handled the Colts like they were an extension of his arms. And fast—God, the boy was fast.

Kirby practiced an hour each day drawing and dry-firing the Colts. In only a matter of weeks, his draw had become a blur—too fast for the eye to follow. And he was deadly accurate.

Well, Emmett mused, making up his mind, he was glad they had run into Preacher, and he was glad the mountain man had taken such an interest in Kirby. Smoke, he amended that. He was also glad the boy could take care of himself in a bad situation. For, although the father had not told the son, the move westward had not been pure impulse. Even had his wife not been dead, Emmett would have moved westward . . . he had given his word to Mosby.

If it took him forever, Emmett had sworn to Mosby, he would find and kill three men: Stratton, Potter, and Richards.

And he was sure Preacher had guessed there was a mission to fulfill in the back of the elder Jensen's mind.

Preacher was no fool—he was sharp. Emmett would have to confide in the old man—soon. For the three traitors and murderers, Potter, Stratton, and Richards, had said many times they were going to the place called

Idaho when the war ended. And with the stolen Confederate gold, they would have ample funds to start a business. Ranches, more than likely, although one of them had expressed a desire to open a trading post.

Emmett knew, if he found the men at all, it might take months, even years. But he also knew he didn't have years. But he had to find them. Had to kill them.

Or be killed, he reflected morosely.

While Kirby rode on ahead, his bay prancing, the boy taking to the new land like a colt to a field of clover, Preacher hung back to speak with Emmett, both of them keeping one eye on the boy.

"You got a burr under your saddle, Emmett," Preacher said. "Wanna talk about it?"

"I got things to do. And it might take me some time to do them."

"I figured as much."

"Thought you would have. I took no allegiance to the federal government after Lee surrendered. But I did swear to kill three men and get back as much of the Confederate gold they stole as possible. I'll do it, too."

"War's over," the old man observed. "Who you gonna give the gold to?"

"I might give it to Kirby. Maybe I'll just toss it in the river. Don't know. It's tainted." He looked at Preacher. "You'll take care of my boy?"

"You know that without askin'."

"Teach him what you know?"

"That's my plan. But they's more to this than you're sayin'. You had that cough long?"

"You're pretty sharp, Preacher."

"Don't know about that. Just keep my eyes and ears

open, that's all."

"I caught a ball through the lung. Laid me flat on my back for weeks. Got infected. Then lung fever hit the other lung. Maybe—just maybe—if I stayed in a dry climate, I might make it, according to the doctors. But they didn't sound hopeful. I can't do that. I swore I'd find those men."

"Who are they?"

"Wiley Potter, Josh Richards, and a man named Stratton. They turned traitor and robbed some gold meant to keep the Confederacy going a while longer. That was bad enough, but they killed several men while stealing the gold. One of the men killed was my son, Luke."

Preacher grunted. "Smoke know about that?"

"No. He thinks his brother was killed fighting with Lee, in the wilderness. If I don't come back from this, you tell him the truth, all right?"

"Done."

"I'll be pulling out after I stock up with some supplies in Pueblo. I'll tell Kirby all I think he needs to know."

Kirby stood in front of the trading post at dawn, watching his father ride out, pack horse trailing. Emmett had taken only a few of the gold coins, leaving the rest with Kirby. The young man was conscious of the weight of the coins in the leather bag around his neck. His father stopped, spun his horse, and waved at his son. Kirby returned the wave, then his Pa was gone, dipping out of sight, over the rise of a small hill.

Preacher sat on the porch of the trading post,

watching, saying nothing. Kirby turned, looking at the man who was to become his mentor.

"Will he be back?" The boy's voice was shaky.

"Ifn he can." Preacher spat on the dusty ground. "Some things, Smoke, a man's just gotta do 'fore his time on earth slips away. Your Pa has things to do. Smoke, ifn you wanna cry—and they ain't no shame in a man cryin'—best go 'round back and do it. Get it over with."

Kirby squared his shoulders. "I'm a man," he said, his voice firming. "I lived alone and worked the land and paid the taxes—all by myself. I haven't cried since Ma died."

Lot of weight on a boy's shoulders, Preacher thought. "Well, then, we'd best buy some salt and flour and beans and sich. Get you outfitted. Then we'll ride on outta here."

"Where will we meet up with Pa?"

"Brown's Hole—ifn he's lucky. Next year. Year after. He'll get word to us."

Kirby put a foot on the steps. "Let's get outfitted."

The man behind the counter at the trading post had given the boy ten dollars for the scalps in his war bag, winking at Preacher as he did so. Kirby had not seen the wink.

Kirby pointed to a shiny new Henry repeating rifle on the rack. "I want one of those," he told the man. "And a hundred rounds of .44s." He took a few coins from the leather bag. "For the Henry, I'll trade you this Spencer and pay the difference. Whatever is fair."

Man and boy haggled for fifteen minutes, the man finally throwing up his arms in an exaggerated gesture of surrender. The transaction was done.

Kirby bought an extra cylinder for his left hand .36, and a sack full of powder and shot.

They rode out.

Preacher told him he knew of a friendly band of Injuns up north of the post a ways. He'd see to it that Smoke got hisself a pair of moccasins and leggings and a buckskin jacket—fancy beaded.

"I ain't got that kind of money to waste, Preacher."

"Ain't gonna cost you nothin'. I know the lady who'll make 'em."

"She must like you pretty well."

Preacher smiled. "She's my daughter."

September, 1865

The pair rode easily but carefully through the towering mountains and lush timber. They had once again crossed the Arkansas and were now almost directly between Mt. Elbert to the north, and Mt. Harvard to the south. They had nooned and nighted just outside a small trading post on the banks of the Arkansas—which would later become the town of Buena Vista—and picked up bacon and beans and coffee. They had left before dawn, both of them seeking the solitude of the high lonesome. It had not taken Kirby long to fall prey to the lure of the lonesome. The country was wild and beautiful, and except for Indians, sparsely populated.

"Where're we headin'?" Kirby asked.

"In a round 'bout way, to one of my cabins. On the North Fork. We'll have to winter there. It's gonna be a bad one, too."

Kirby looked around him. The day was pleasant, but cool. "How can you tell that this early?"

"Leaves on the aspen. Whenever they start turnin' gold this early in the fall, the winter's gonna be a bitch-kitty. Bet on it. But we'll have things to do, Smoke. Hunt, run traps, chop wood, and," he said grinning, "stay alive. That there is the mainest thing."

"Sometimes I get the feeling we're the first white men to see this country, Preacher."

"Know the feelin' well. But they's mountain men through here 'fore I was born. And not too many years ago an army man, named Gunnison, Captain Gunnison, as I recall, came through here. That was back in '52 or '53. He was chartin' the land."

"For what?"

"Railroad, I heared." He spat his contempt on the ground.

"When they gonna build it?"

"Not in my lifetime, I hope. I don't wanna see this here country all tore up. Pilgrims comin' in with their plows, a-draggin' they wimmin and squallin' kids with 'em." He shuddered. "Damn nuisance. Makes my skin crawl."

Kirby grinned. "That could be fleas, Preacher."

"Watch your mouth, boy—don't sass an old man."

Kirby laughed with his friend. "Some people might call the railroad progress, Preacher."

"Some people might paint wings on a pig and try to make it fly, too. No, sir. Land oughtta be left the way God made it. Already folk in here pokin' holes in the ground, lookin' for gold and silver. They scarin' off the game, makin' the Injuns mad at ever'body. It's a damn shame and a dis-grace."

"Preacher?"

"Yep, Smoke."

"What happened back at the fort. Bent's Fort, I mean. Did the Indians destroy it?"

"Nope. Old Bent blew it up hisself. That was back in . . . oh . . . . '52, I think."

They stopped, allowing their horses to drink and blow.

"Blew up his own fort? That's crazy. Why would he do that?"

Preacher chuckled. "Old Bill Bent was probably one of the finest men I ever knowed. I guess he just got discouraged when the fur trade kind of petered out. That'us back about '50. He tried to sell the fort to the government, but they fiddle-faddled around for two years tryin' to make up they minds. Far as I'm concerned, ain't been nobody in government had a mind since Crockett. Anyways, ol' Bill just blowed the damn thing up, loaded his goods on wagons, and moved down the Arkansas to Short Timber Crick. He set up two-three more places, but they weren't none of 'em nearabouts as grand as the first."

Kirby had gotten lost in the big hotel in Springfield; that was grand. He couldn't imagine anything to match that out here.

"Yes, sir, Smoke, Bent's Fort had nice livin' quarters, a bar, and a billiard room. That there bar served up a drink called Taos Lightning. And let me tell you, it were ever'thing it was cracked up to be. Struck your stomach like a fulminate cap to powder."

The old man and the young man rode on, climbing higher, the air cool as it pulled at their lungs. They rode for an hour without speaking, content to be surrounded by God's handiwork.

"Where is Mr. Bent now, Preacher?"

"Don't rightly know, Smoke. He were married two times—that I know of. Both times to Injun wimmin. First wife died . . . can't 'member her name. Then old Bill hitched up with her sister, Yellow Woman. Last I heared, he was livin' with one of his kids, on the Purgatoire River.

"Is he a legend?"

"Damn shore is. Just like you will be, Smoke. Someday."

The young man laughed. "I'll never be a legend, Preacher."

"Yeah, you will." Preacher's reply was solemn. "I can see it all around you, in ever'thing you do."

"Well, I guess only time will prove that, Preacher."

"As much time as the Good Lord gives you, Smoke."

FIVE

That winter of 1865/66 was a brutal one, with days of snow that sometimes piled up to the shuttered windows of the cabin along the banks of the North Fork.

With time on his hands, Kirby read and reread, many times, the McGuffey's reader his father had bought for him. And he found, much to his surprise, that Preacher had a dozen or so thick volumes, including the selected works of a man called Shakespeare.

"I didn't know you read, Preacher," Kirby said, the howl of the winter winds muffled inside the small, snug cabin.

"Don't. Can't read airy word. But I wintered once with a feller who, as it turned out, had been a school teacher back East. Them books belonged to him."

"Belonged?"

"Thought hisself quite a ladies' man, that feller did. 'Bout twenty year ago—give or take some—he took a shinin' to a squaw over the mountain east of here. Only problem was that there squaw already had herself a buck, and that Injun didn't much cotton to that school teacher makin' eyes at his woman. He caught 'em together one afternoon. They was . . . ah . . ."

Kirby got his hopes up. At last!

". . . kissin' and things."

Damn! "What things?"

"Things. Don't interrupt. That buck killed the school teacher, cut off the woman's nose, and kicked 'er out. I got left with the books and the body. Buried the body. Didn't know what to do with the books, so I kept 'em. Used to be more'un them there. Rats et 'em over the years."

"Cut off her nose!"

"Injun way of divorce, you might call it. It varies from tribe to tribe."

"What happens to the man if he's unfaithful to the woman?"

"Some tribes, the woman can kick him and his goods right out of the wickiup, and he ain't got no say in the matter—none a-tall."

"Seems fair," the young man observed.

"Some bucks might not agree with you," Preacher said with a smile. "'Pecially this time of year."

The Chinook winds blew once in the late winter of '66, melting the snow and creating a false illusion of spring, confusing the vegetation and the animals. The warm winds also brought a stirring within the boy/man called Smoke.

"It ain't gonna last," Preacher told Kirby, now in his

seventeenth year. "Likely be a blizzard tomorrow. Relax, Smoke, spring'll be here 'fore you know it." The mountain smiled knowingly. "You act like you got the juices runnin' in you."

"What do you mean?"

Preacher cocked an eye at him. "Girls, boy. You know."

Kirby shook his head. "No, sir. I don't know nothin' about girls."

Preacher paled.

"I figured you'd tell me about females."

"Lord Gawd!"

"You mean I have to ask *Him*!"

"Don't blaspheme, young man," Preacher said sternly. "Come a time—and this ain't the time," he was quick to add, "you'll learn all there is for a man to know 'bout females." He grimaced. "And a bunch you don't want to know. Most aggravatin' creatures God ever put on this here earth. Can't live with 'em, can't do without 'em."

"That's what my father used to say. But he'd always grin at Ma when he said it."

"He better grin," Preacher replied.

Kirby read for a time while Preacher slept by the fire. When Preacher awoke, Kirby asked, "What do we do when spring does get here?" His thoughts were suddenly flung far, to his father, wondering where he was, if he was still alive.

"I start learnin' you good. And you start bein' a man."

"I wonder where my Pa is?"

"He's either on the way to doin' what he set out to do; he's already done 'er, or he's doin' it."

"Or he's dead," Kirby added.

"Mayhaps," Preacher's words were soft. "We all get to see the elephant someday."

"I don't know the whole story, Preacher. Pa said you'd tell me when it was time. I reckon it ain't time just yet."

"That's so, Smoke."

"All right. But I'll tell you this, Preacher: If those men he went after killed him, I'll track them down, one by one, and I'll kill them. And anyone who gets in my way." His words did not come from the lips of a boy; but a man grown in many ways.

Preacher had a sudden flash of precognition, the foreseeing coming hard, chilling the old mountain man.

"Yep," he said. "I reckon you will, Smoke."

The warm winds once again blew, and this time they were the real advance guard of spring. First to show their appreciation of the cycle of renewal were the peonies, bursting forth in a cacophony of color. The columbine, which would one day be the official flower of the yet-to-be-admitted state of Colorado, cast forth its contribution to spring, in colors of blue and lavender and purple and white. The valleys and foothills, the plains and mountains exploded in a holiday of technicolor.

And on that day, Preacher packed his gear and told his young friend to do the same. "Walls closin' in. Time to get movin'. Time for you to start learnin'."

With their Henry repeating rifles across their

saddles, the pair rode out, heading northeast from the North Fork, into the timber and the mountains. Still, one hour each day, the boy called Smoke practiced with his deadly Colts, perfecting what some would later write was not only the first fast draw, but the fastest draw.

Those few who would get to know the man called Smoke would say he was even faster than the legendary Texas gunfighter, John Wesley Hardin; possessing more cold nerve than Wild Bill; meaner than Curly Bill; and as much a hand with the ladies as Sundance. But for now, Kirby was learning, and the mountain man taught him well.

Still spry as a cat and tougher than wang-leather, Preacher taught Kirby fistfighting and boxing and Indian wrestling. But more importantly, he taught him to win in a fight—and taught him that it didn't make a damn how you won. Just win. He taught him to kick, gouge, throw, and bite.

"Long as you right, Smoke, it don't make no difference how you win. Just be sure you in the right."

"Not knowin' the land and the animals can get a body dead," Preacher told him. "I'll start like you don't know nothin'. Which is not that far from the truth. Snakes."

"Huh?"

"Snakes. Tell me what you know 'bout 'em."

"I know to leave some of them alone."

"Wise, but not near enough."

"Well . . . I know a poisonous snake's got to coil

before they strike."

"Wrong. A rattler can short-strike at you with just the power of his neck. You 'member that. And this, too: Rattler meat is good to eat. I've et a poke of it. Right tasty. But be damn shore the critter is dead 'fore you start to skin it. They get right hostile ifn you's to jerk the hide off 'fore they's dead."

Kirby smiled. "Wouldn't you?"

Preacher laughed. "'Spect so. Injuns was gonna skin me alive one time, up on the Platte. That's how I got my name, Preacher. I preached to them heathens for hours. Didn't think I knowed so many words. Even made me up a language that day and night. Called it the unknown tongue. But I made believers out of them savages. I reckon they thought I was crazy. Injuns won't harm a crazy man—most of 'em, that is. They think he's kind of a God. Finally that chief just put his hands over his ears and told his bucks to turn me a-loose. Said I's a hurtin' his ears something fierce. I got my pelts and rode out of there without lookin' back." He chuckled at the long-ago memory.

"And you've been called Preacher ever since."

"Yep."

Preacher had blindfolded the young man and spun him around like a top. Removing the sash, Preacher asked, "Which direction you facin', Smoke?"

Kirby shook his head, looking around him. "North."

"Wrong. You looked at that moss on yonder tree, didn't you?"

"Yes, sir."

"That kind of thinkin' can get you kilt. Moss, ifn there's light and water enough, can grow all the way 'round a tree. Man can wander 'round in circles and die believin' that moss only grows to the north."

"Then—"

Preacher answered the unspoken question. "Sun, stars, lay of the land, and a feel for them all. Come a time, Smoke, you'll just know. It won't take long."

The days passed into weeks, and Kirby's education grew, and so did he, gaining weight, filling out with hard muscle.

The young man pointed his finger at a bush full of berries. "I know about them—we got them in Missouri. Don't eat them, they're poison."

Preacher grinned. "But some birds do."

"Yes. But you said not to believe that old story that anything a bird eats a man can eat."

"That's right. See them flowers over yonder. Right purty and lots of birds eat 'em. But they can kill a man, or else make him so sick he'll wish he was dead. Oak tree yonder. I've knowed folk to boil the bark and make a bitter-tastin' tonic. Never cared for the stuff myself."

"Why?"

"'Cause it tastes like pisen water. And I just don't care to drink no pisen water."

As they traveled, they would occasionally encounter roaming bands of Indians, most of them friendly to Preacher. Once, after they had palavered with a band of Cheyenne, Kirby looked back in time to see one of the braves making a circling motion at his temple with a forefinger. He told Preacher.

"Sure. Sign for a crazy person. Let 'em keep believin' it. We'll keep our hair."

"Why do Indians think a crazy person is a God?"

"Well, they believe he's possessed by gods—nearabout the same thing to them. And the Injuns don't want no bad medicine with no God.

"They don't worship like we do, Smoke. Injun worships the sun, the stars, the trees, the moon, the rivers. Nearabouts ever'thing. Least the Injuns I know does. They can't rightly tell you why they think a man crazy is thataway. I've heared twelve different versions from twelve different medicine men. Don't none of 'em make no sense to me."

During their wanderings, they met trappers and hunters, a few of whom rode from the west. Kirby would always ask about Emmett. But no one had seen him or heard about him. It was as if the man had dropped off the face of the earth.

"Idaho is wild, Smoke," Preacher told him. "Only a few places settled. We ain't heard nothin' by next spring, we'll strike out for the Hole."

1867

The pair spent the winter of 1866/67 in an old cabin on the banks of the Colorado River, with the northern slopes of Castle Peak far to the south, but visible on most days. Here, the pair ran traps, hunted, and on the bitter cold days and nights, stayed snug in the cabin built some forty years earlier by a long dead friend of Preacher's.

"What happened to the man who built this cabin?"

"He got tied up with a mountain lion one afternoon," Preacher said. "The puma won."

In the spring of '67, they sold their pelts at a post and rode out for the northwest.

"Show you where we used to rendezvous, Smoke. Back 'bout '30, I think it were. Worst damn place I ever been in my life. We called it Fort Misery. First time I ever et dog. Warn't too bad as I recall."

Kirby shuddered. "You've eaten dog since?"

"Shore. Many times. And so will you. That's why Injuns keep so many dogs 'round they camp. Come winter, food gets scarce, they cook up dog. It's right good."

Kirby hoped he would never eat dog. "This Brown's Hole—that where we're headin'?"

"Yep. On the Utah side of Brown's Hole, just west of Wild Canyon. Quiet there. I told your Pa 'bout it. Said ifn he could, he'd meet us there—somehow."

Kirby didn't like the sound of—somehow.

They had taken their time, riding through the Flat Tops Primitive area, past Sleepy Cat Peak, and into the Danforth Hills. They made camp at the confluence of the Little Snake and Yampa Rivers—and they stayed put for three weeks.

"What are we waiting for?" Kirby asked impatiently, the youth in him overriding his near manhood.

"Somebody'll be along directly." Preacher calmed him. "They always is. So you just hold your water, Smoke—we got time."

At the end of the third week, a mountain man rode in. He looked, at least to Kirby, to be as old as God.

"You just as ugly as I 'membered, Preacher," he said, in a form of greeting.

Kirby had learned that mountain men insulted each other whenever possible. It was their way of showing affection.

"You should talk, Grizzly," Preacher retorted. "I 'member what Elk Man told you thirty year ago: You could hire out your face to scare little children."

A pained look crossed the old man's face. "Hell, Preacher," he said in mock indignation, "I didn't ride seventy mile to get insulted."

"'Course you did. I'm one of the few that can stand to look at you. Light and sit, we got grub."

"You cook it?"

"Hell, yes, I cooked it!"

"That's even a worst insult," Grizzly said. But he dismounted, dropped the reins on the ground, and filled a plate with food.

After his second helping, piling his plate high with venison, wild potatoes mixed with wild onions, and gravy, the old mountain man wiped his tin plate clean with a piece of Kirby's panbread, then poured a third cup of coffee. He belched contentedly and patted his stomach. "Bread was good, anyways. Boy must have made that."

Preacher glared at him. "I'd druther have to buy your traps than feed you for any length of time. You eat like a hog."

Preacher and Grizzly insulted one another for a full half hour, each one trying to outdo the other. Kirby had never heard such tall tales and wild insults. The men finally agreed it was a draw.

Grizzly said, "Do I talk in front of the boy?"

"He ain't no boy. He's a growed man."

Kirby poured himself a cup of coffee and waited.

"Man rode into the Hole 'bout two months ago. All shot up. Had a bad cough. He—"

"Is he still alive?" Kirby blurted.

Grizzly turned cold eyes on the young man. "Don't never 'rupt a man when he's a-palaverin'. Tain't polite. One thing 'bout Injuns, they know manners. They gonna 'low a man to speak his piece without 'ruptin'. 'Course they might skin you alive the minute you finished, but they ain't gonna 'rupt you while you's talkin'."

"Sorry," Kirby said.

"'Cepted. No, he's dead. Strange man. Dug his own grave. Come the time, I buried him. He's planted on that there little plain on the base of the high peak, east side of the canyon. You 'member it, Preacher?"

Preacher nodded.

Grizzly reached inside his war bag and pulled out a heavy sack. He tossed the sack to Kirby. "This be yourn, from your Pa. Right smart 'mount of gold." Again, he dipped into the buckskin and beaded bag, pulling out a rawhide-wrapped flat object. "This here is a piece of paper with words on it. Names, your Pa said, of the men who put lead in him. He said you'd know what to do, but for me to tell you don't do nothin' rash." Grizzly rose to his feet. "I done what I gave my word I'd do. Now I'll be goin'. Thankee both for the grub."

Without another word, the old mountain man mounted his pony, gathered his pack horses, and rode off east. He did not look back.

"Ain't no point in movin' now," Preacher said. "Be dark in three hours. We'll pull out at first light."

At eighteen, Kirby had achieved his full growth: six feet, two inches tall, packing a hundred and eighty pounds of bone and muscle. His shoulders, arms, and hands were powerful, his legs long, his waist lean. His hair was long and ash-blond. His hands and face were deeply tanned. His eyes were an unreadable brown.

The bay his father had given him had not survived the first winter, slipping on ice and breaking a leg, forcing Kirby to shoot the animal. He now rode a tough mountain horse he had traded from an Indian, a huge Appaloosa, much larger than most of that breed. The Indian had ridden away chuckling, thinking he had gotten the better of the deal, for the Appaloosa would allow no one to ride it, refusing to be broken. But Kirby had slow-gentled the animal, bringing it along slowly and carefully, step by step. Now, no one but Kirby could put a saddle on the animal, much less ride him. He was a stallion, and he was mean, his eyes warning any knowledgeable person away. The Appaloosa had, in addition to its distinctive markings, the mottled hide, vertically striped hoofs, and pale eyes, a perfectly shaped seven between his eyes. And that became his name. Seven.

Gone was the McClellen saddle, replaced by a western rig, slightly heavier, but much more comfortable.

Smoke and Seven.

Emmett's horses had been picketed close to the base of Zenobia Peak. His gear was by his grave, covered with a ground sheet and secured with rocks. There were several more horses than Emmett had left with.

"You read them words on that paper your Pa left you?" Preacher asked.

"Not yet."

"I'll go set up camp at the Hole. I reckon you'll be along directly."

"Tomorrow. 'Bout noon."

"See you then." Preacher headed north. He would cross Vermillion Creek, then cut west into the Hole. Smoke would find him when he felt ready for human company. But for now, the young man needed to be alone with his Pa.

Kirby unsaddled Seven, allowing him to roll. He stripped the gear from the pack animals, setting them grazing. He picketed only the pack animals, for Seven would not stray far from him.

Taking a small hammer and a miner's spike from his gear, Kirby began the job of chiseling his father's name into a large, flat rock. He could not remember exactly when his Pa was born, but thought it about 1815.

Headstone in place, secured by heavy rocks, Kirby built his small fire, put coffee on to boil in the blackened pot, then sat down to read the letter from his Pa.

"Son,

I found some of the men who killed your brother,

Luke, and stolt the gold that belonged to the Gray. Theys more of them than I first thought. I killed two of the men work for them, but they got led in me and I had to hitail it out. Came here. Not goin to make it. Son, you dont owe nuttin to the Cause of the Gray. So dont get it in your mind you do. Make yoursalf a good life and look to my restin place if you need help.

Preacher kin tell you some of what happen, but not all. Remember: look to my grave if you need help.

I allso got word that your sis, Janey, leff that gambler and has took up with an outlaw down in Airyzona. Place called Tooson. I woodn fret much about her. She is mine, but I think she is trash. Dont know where she got that streek from.

I am gettin tared and seein is hard. Lite fadin. I love you Kirby-Smoke.

Pa."

Kirby reread the letter. *Look to my grave.* He could not understand that part. He pulled up his knees and his head on them, feeling he ought to cry, or something. But no tears came.

Now he was alone. He had no other kin, and he did not count his sister as kin. He had his guns, his horses, a bit of gold, and his friend, Preacher.

He was eighteen years old.

SIX

1869

Having been born and reared on a farm, the earth was naturally a part of Kirby. So on the Utah side of the Hole, the tall young man planted several gardens: corn, beans, greens, potatoes. All carefully irrigated from a small stream. Preacher had scoffed at this, saying, "I'd be gawddamned ifn I'd bust any sod!" But Kirby noticed the old man ate up the vegetables on his plate, and usually helped himself to seconds, sometimes thirds.

Kirby had caught up with a band of wild horses, mustangs with some Appaloosa mixed in, and started raising horses. He now had a respectable herd.

Kirby no longer practiced with his Colts. He did not need to practice. He was a crack shot and blindingly fast.

Preacher, now pushing hard into his sixty-eighth

year, was just as spry as when Kirby had first laid eyes on him—and just as cantankerous and ornery.

Kirby laid claim to all the land between Vermillion Creek to the east, and about two sections past the still ill-defined Utah state line to the west. All the land from Diamond Peak to the north, down to and including Brown's Hole. He rode once to a small town about a hundred and fifty miles from the Hole and filed on his claim. But the town died out a year later, becoming yet another ghost town on the western landscape, and Kirby's claim was never recognized in the years ahead. It was illegal from the outset, since he was claiming far too much land, but Kirby figured—and figured correctly—that since the land was so desolate and in some instances, downright barren, no one else would want it.

Tucked away in the far reaches of the northwestern part of Colorado, Kirby and Preacher lived alone—and became something of a mystery, much as the hermit, Pat Lynch would someday become. Pat, who later lived in the canyon with a pet mountain lion named Jenny Lind. Kirby and Preacher were not talkative men, sometimes going for days without speaking.

A wild and raging canyon cut down from the Hole: the Green River. It would later be named Lodore Canyon, by an army major, a geologist who was fond of quoting the poet Southey's "How The Waters Come Down At Lodore," as he shot the rapids.

Emmett Jensen's grave was now covered with a profusion of wild flowers, clinging stubbornly to the rocky soil. Kirby visited the grave weekly, sometimes standing for hours by the site. He spoke silently to his

Pa, wishing he knew what to do. He always left with a mild feeling of discontent, as if he should be doing *something* about the men who killed his Pa.

At first, Preacher had told him, "You just too young yet to do much of anything 'bout them men who kilt your Pa. You got all the makin's, but you still need some seasonin'. Give it time, Smoke. Them folk be there when you ready to make your move."

But as the months marched into a year, then two, Preacher knew the boy was gone, and in its place, a man grown. He knew, too, from his half century and more on the trail, that the young man called Smoke was a potentially dangerous man: big and solid and steady and strong as a bear. A man whose draw with those old Navy Colts was so fast as to be a blur. And he never missed. Never.

The old mountain man knew little of the emotion called love. He had liked the squaws he had wintered with, sharing their buffalo robes—liked them all. He had enjoyed playing with his children. And somewhere in the back of his mind, he held a memory of his mother: a faded, time-worn retention of the woman, but without a clear face. He knew he must have loved her as a child. But the call of the open plains, the wilderness, the unknown, the high lonesome, the untraveled hills and mountains and trails, had been too much; overpowering love.

But with the man he called Smoke, the mountain man knew what he felt must be love, for in Smoke was everything the old man would want in a son: strength, daring, courage, eager to face the unknown, willing to learn, to pit himself against the wilderness. Then, finally, the old man admitted the truth: He did not want Smoke to face the men on that list—for fear of losing him. He had been deliberately holding him back.

And that ain't right, he concluded. *The man is twenty year old,* Preacher thought. *Time to cut loose the tie-string and let him taste the world of people. He ain't gonna like it—just like me—but he got to see for hisself.*

The rattle of sabers and the pounding of hoofs broke into Preacher's ruminations.

"Men comin'!" he called.

The young man known but to a few white men as Smoke stepped out of the cabin. His guns, as always, belted around his waist, the right hand Colt hanging lower than the butt-forward left gun. Had there been a woman with the detachment of cavalry, she would have called the young man handsome, and her heart might have beat just a bit faster, for he was striking-looking.

"Hello!" the officer in charge called. "I was not aware this area was inhabited by white men."

"You is now," Preacher said shortly.

"My name is Major John Wesley Powell, United States Army."

"I'm Preacher. This here is Smoke. An' now that we know each other, why don't you leave?"

The major laughed good-naturedly. "Why, sir, we've come to do a bit of exploring."

His good humor was not returned by either man. "What do you want to know 'bout this country?" Preacher asked. "Just name it, and I'll tell you—save you a mess of trouble. Then you can leave."

"May we dismount?"

"Dismount, sit, squat, stand, or kick your heels up in the air. It don't make no difference to me."

Major Powell laughed openly, heartily, then dismounted, telling his sergeant to have the men dismount and stand easy. "You old mountain men never cease to amaze me. And I mean that as a compliment," he added. His eyes turned to Kirby. "But you're far too young to have been a mountain man. Are you men related?"

"I'm his son," Preacher said with a straight face. "He fell in the Fountain of Youth a few years back, but he bumped his head doin' it and now he can't recall where it is. I'm waitin'."

Preacher glanced at the old scout with the army and then looked away.

"I got things to tell you, Preacher," the scout said.

"All right."

"Well," the major said with a smile. He cleared his throat. "Tell me, what do either of you men know about the river that flows through the canyon?"

"It's wet," Kirby said.

"And it ain't no place for a pilgrim," Preacher added.

"Then I take it that both of you have traversed the Green River?"

Preacher looked at Kirby for translation.

"Been down it," Kirby said.

"Hell yes, I been down it," Preacher said. "I been down it, up it, through it, crost it, and one time, back in '39, over it."

"The only man to ever shoot those rapids," a young lieutenant contradicted, "was General Ashley, back in '23 and '24."

"Yeah," Kirby said. "His name's still on the rock on the eastern side of the canyon wall. And don't never again call Preacher a liar."

The young officer stirred until the major called him softly down. "Stand easy, Robert." In a lower voice, heard only by a sergeant and the young officer, he said, "This is your first tour of duty out here, Bob—you know nothing of western men. Until you learn more about the customs here, it would behoove you to curb your tongue. Calling a man a liar, or merely inferring he is one, is a shooting matter west of the Mississippi. This is not Philadelphia, so just be quiet." He looked at Kirby. "He meant no offense, Mr. Smoke."

"Not mister—just Smoke."

"Unusual name," the major remarked.

"I give it to him," Preacher said. "After he kilt his first two men. I think he was fifteen, thereabouts."

The young lieutenant paled slightly.

The major said, "We saw a grave coming in. The name was Jensen."

"My father."

"I'm sorry, sir."

"Not nearly as sorry as the men who killed him will be."

Preacher looked at him. "You make your mind up?"

"About a half an hour ago."

"We goin' after 'em?"

"Yep."

"Figures."

Major stood quietly, not knowing what was going on. "I gather you men live here?"

"I own it," Kirby said.

"Own it? How much of it?"

Kirby told him.

"Why . . . that's hundreds of square miles!"

"We like lots of room."

"You have papers on this?"

"I filed on it, yeah. But I have no objections to you and your men staying here. Just don't trample my gardens or take my horses."

The major had stepped closer, standing by a large, flat rock. "I assure you, sir, we will leave the—"

No one saw the young man draw, cock and pull the trigger of his right hand Colt. It was done as fast as a man could blink. The major looked down: A headless rattlesnake writhed at his boots.

"Sweet Molly!" a young cavalryman said. "I never even seen him draw."

Major Powell was a cool one; he had not moved. He kicked the squirming snake out of the way and said, "That was the most impressive shooting with a handgun I believe I've ever seen. I thank you, Smoke."

"Man can't be too careful out here," Preacher said, a bored look on his bearded face. "I take it upon myself to tell all pilgrims that."

The major smiled at this quiet slur. "I don't believe I've ever seen a man draw, cock, and fire a pistol that quickly. I'm sure I haven't. But I'm told the outlaw, Jesse James, is also quite proficient with a handgun."

"Who?" Kirby was startled.

"Jesse James. The Missouri bank robber and outlaw. Do you know him?"

"I've met him." Kirby drew his right hand Colt and tossed the weapon to the major.

The cavalryman inspected the pistol, noting the initials J J. carved into the handles. Powell tossed the pistol back to Kirby. "I see," he said quietly, not quite certain where he now stood, for emotions concerning the James Gang ran both hot and cold, depending upon which side of the fence one stood. "And where are you from originally, Smoke?"

"That ain't a polite question to ask out here," Preacher informed him.

"I know," the major said. "I shouldn't have asked it. I withdraw it."

"It's all right," Kirby said. "I'm from the southwestern part of Missouri."

"Did you fight in the Civil War?"

"My Pa fought in the War Between the States," Kirby said with a smile.

"Ah . . . yes." The major returned the smile. He would say no more about James. He mounted, ordering his men to do the same. "We shan't disturb you, gentlemen. We'll bivouac on the other side of the canyon. Perhaps we'll see each other again."

"I doubt it," Kirby said.

"Oh?"

"Me and Preacher got things to do and places to go. Any horse you see around here with the SJ brand belongs to us. If you need a horse, take your pick of the mustangs and geldings, leave the mares alone. Just leave the money—what you think they're worth—in the cave at the Hole."

"Thank you," the major said. "You are a trusting man, Smoke."

"Not really. I just believe you don't want to cheat me."

Major Powell sensed in the young man a heavy, almost tangible aura of danger. The dark eyes gave no hint of what lay behind them.

"No," the army officer said. "I don't believe I want to do that."

The cavalrymen were gone in a cloud of dust, all but the old buckskin-clad scout who had guided them to this old post. He had not dismounted. He looked at Preacher.

"Thought you's dead," he finally said.

Preacher glared at him. "Yeah? That's what you get for tryin' to stir up that mess between your ears."

The scout grunted. "Walked right into that, I reckon." He shifted his gaze to Kirby. "Met a man who knowed your Pa in the war. One of Mosby's people. All stove up now—livin' over to the hot springs on the San Juan. Valley there. He heared 'bout your Pa gettin' lead in him west of here. His name is Gaultier. Don't ask me to spell it. He might know something that you wanna know. Told him I'd tell you ifn I saw you. I seen you. I told you. Good seein' you agin, Preacher."

"Right nice seein' you, Rio."

The scout wheeled his horse and was gone.

"Friend of yours?" Kirby asked.

"Not so's you'd know it. We fought over the same squaw back in '49. He lost. We ain't had much to do with each other since then. He's a sore loser."

"Can we trust him?"

"Oh, yeah. We don't cotton to one another, but you can trust him."

"Want to take a ride to the springs?"

"What do you think?"

Pagosa Springs, which translated means Indian healing waters, lies at the bottom of the state, not far from the New Mexico line, in what would someday become the San Juan National Forest. Several hundred miles, as the crow flies, from Brown's Hole, through some of the roughest and most beautiful country in the state. Late summer when the two men reached the hot springs. Preacher had groused and bitched the entire way.

"Gawddamned farmers! I never seen so many pilgrims in all my life."

They had seen half a dozen farms in a month.

For Preacher, it was his first encounter with barbed wire. He had cut his hand, ripped his shirt, and finally fell down before getting loose from the sharp tangle.

Kirby had sat his saddle and laughed at Preacher's antics, which only made matters worse and the profanity more intense.

Just east of the Uncompaghre Plateau, an irritated farmer's wife had threatened both of them with a double-barreled shotgun before Kirby could convince her they meant no harm to her, her pigs, or her kids.

"Woman!" Preacher had railed at her. "You put down that cannon. Why . . . I opened up this country. I—"

She waved the shotgun at him. "Get away from me, you dirty old man."

"Dirty old man! Why you lard-butt heifer, I—"

She stuck the Greener under his beard. "Git!" she commanded.

Preacher was fuming as they rode away. "Damned ole biddy," he cursed. "No respect for my kind. None a-tall."

Kirby grinned. "Civilization is upon us, Preacher."

Preacher violently and heatedly put together a long string of words which profanely contradicted his nickname.

They had stopped at mid-morning just west of the Needle Mountains to replenish their supplies. A wild, roaring mining camp that would soon be named Rico. It was an outlaw hangout in the early 1870s and would continue to be rough and rowdy until almost the turn of the century.

The population of the as yet unnamed settlement had rapidly diminished due to recent Indian raids, but there were still about a hundred men and half a dozen prostitutes in the camp when Kirby and Preacher dismounted in front of the trading post/saloon. As was his custom, Kirby slipped the thongs from the hammers of his Colts at dismounting.

They bought their supplies and turned to leave when the hum of conversation suddenly died. Two rough-dressed and unshaven men, both wearing guns, blocked the door.

"Who owns that horse out there?" one demanded, a snarl to his voice, trouble in his manner. "The one with an SJ brand?"

Kirby laid his purchases on the counter. "I do," he said quietly.

"Which way'd you ride in from?"

Preacher had slipped to the right, his left hand covering the hammer of his Henry, concealing the click as he thumbed it back.

Kirby faced the men, his right hand hanging loose by his side. His left hand was just inches from his left hand gun. "Who wants to know—and why?"

No one in the dusty building moved or spoke.

"Pike's my name," the bigger and uglier of the pair said. "And I say you came through my diggin's yesterday and stole my dust."

"And I say you're a liar," Kirby told him.

Pike grinned nastily, his right hand hovering near the butt of his pistol. "Why . . . you little pup. I think I'll shoot your ears off."

"Why don't you try? I'm sure tired of hearing you shoot your mouth off."

Pike looked puzzled for a few seconds; bewilderment crossed his features. No one had ever talked to him in this manner. Pike was big, strong, and a bully. "I think I'll just kill you for that."

Pike and his partner reached for their guns.

Four shots boomed in the low-ceilinged room. Four shots so closely spaced they seemed as one thunderous roar. Dust and bird's nest droppings fell from the ceiling. Pike and his friend were slammed out the open doorway. One fell off the rough porch, dying in the dirt street. Pike, with two holes in his chest, died with his back to a support pole, his eyes still open, unbelieving. Neither had managed to pull a pistol more than halfway out of leather.

All eyes in the black powder-filled and dusty, smoky room moved to the young man standing by the bar, a Colt in each hand. "Good God!" a man whispered in awe. "I never even seen the draw."

Preacher had moved the muzzle of his Henry to cover the men at the tables. The bartender put his hands slowly on the bar, indicating he wanted no trouble.

"We'll be leaving now," Kirby said, holstering his

Colts and picking up his purchases from the counter. He walked out the open door.

Kirby stepped over the sprawled, dead legs of Pike and walked past his dead friend.

"What are we 'posed to do with the bodies?" a man asked Preacher.

"Bury 'em."

"What's that kid's name?"

"Smoke."

They camped deep in the big timber that night, beside a rushing mountain stream, with the earth for a bed and the stars for a canopy. Over a supper of fresh-caught trout, Preacher asked, "How do you feel, Smoke?"

The young man glanced at his friend, a puzzled look in his eyes. "Why—I feel just fine, Preacher. How come you asked that?"

"You just kilt two men back yonder, Smoke. In front of twelve-fifteen salty ol' boys. And all they could do was a-gape at you with they mouths hangin' open. Now I ain't sayin' Pike and his friend didn't need killin', 'cause they did. They was bullies and troublemakers and trash. Pike's been in these mountains for years and he ain't worth spit. But the point I's makin' is this: Right now the story is being told in that there camp; tomorry night it'll be told 'round a dozen fires. This time next month, it'll be stretched to where you kilt five men, and that's where the salt gets spread on the cut."

"You mean I'll have a reputation?"

"Perzactly. And then ever' two-bit kid who thinks

he's a gun-hand will be lookin' for you, to make a name for hisself."

"They'll never do it from the front."

"You that shore of yourself?"

"Yes, I am."

Preacher laid down his plate and poured a cup of coffee. "Yep, I reckon you is, at that."

SEVEN

THE MAN CALLED SMOKE

It was obvious to even the most uninitiated in medicine that Gaultier did not have much time left on this earth—in his present form.

"Cancer," he told them bluntly. "That's what the doctors say—and I believe them. Waters here help the pain, but I'm not going to make it." He looked at Smoke. "You have your father's eyes. And word is out that you are very good—perhaps the best—with a handgun."

"So I'm told," Smoke said.

"Well, you'd better be," the dying man said matter-of-factly. "Two of Pike's friends rode in yesterday afternoon. One claims to be his brother. Seems they tracked you southeast, then cut around, out of the wilderness, and came in from the south. Thompson and Haywood."

The young man remained calm. "I'm not worried

about them. I'll deal with them when they confront me. What about the men who killed my father?"

Gaultier grinned. "You are a cool one, *jeune homme*. All right. I will tell you about your father—and your brother."

Smoke stepped out of Gaultier's tent along the creek an hour before sunset. He walked down the rutted street, the sun at his back—the way he planned it. Thompson and Haywood were in the big tent at the end of the street, which served as saloon and cafe. Preacher had pointed them out earlier and asked if Smoke needed his help. Smoke said no. The refusal came as no surprise.

As he walked down the street, a man glanced up, spotted him, then hurried quickly inside.

Smoke felt no animosity toward the men in the tent saloon; no anger, no hatred. But they came here after him, so let the dance begin.

The word had swept through the makeshift town, and from behind cabin walls, trees, and boulders. The people watched as Smoke stopped about fifty feet from the tent.

"Haywood! Thompson! You want to see me? Then step out and see me."

The two men pushed back the tent flap and stepped out, both of them angling to get a better look at the man they had tracked. "You the kid called Smoke?" one said.

"I am." With instinct born into a natural fighter, Smoke knew this would be no contest. Both men carried their guns tucked behind wide leather belts; an awkward position from which to draw, for one must first pull the hand up, then over, grabbing the pistol, cocking it as it is pulled from behind the belt, then leveling it to fire. It is also a dandy way to shoot oneself in the belly or side.

"Pike was my brother," the heavier and uglier of the pair said. "And Shorty was my pal."

"You should choose your friends more carefully," Smoke told him.

"They was just a-funnin' with you," Thompson said.

"You weren't there. You don't know what happened."

"You callin' me a liar?"

"If that is the way you want to take it."

Thompson's face colored with anger, his hand moving closer to the .44 in his belt. "You take that back or make your play."

"There is no need for this," Smoke said.

The second man began cursing Smoke as he stood tensely, almost awkwardly, legs spread wide, body bent at the waist. "You're a damned thief. You stolt their gold and then kilt 'em."

Smoke, who had spent hundreds of hours practicing his deadly skills, thought that they were doing everything wrong. These men weren't gun-hands. He could smell the fear-sweat from the men.

"I don't want to have to kill you," Smoke said.

"The kid's yellow!" Haywood yelled. Then he grabbed for his gun.

Haywood touched the butt of his gun just as two shots boomed over the dusty street. The .36 caliber balls struck him in the chest, one nicking his heart.

Haywood dropped to the dirt, dying. Before he closed his eyes, and death relieved him of the shocking pain, closing her arms around him, pulling him into that long sleep, two more shots thundered. He had a dark vision of Thompson spinning in the street. Then Haywood died.

Thompson was on one knee, his left hand holding his shattered right elbow. His leg was bloody. Smoke had knocked his gun from his hand, then shot him in the leg on the way down.

"Pike was your brother," Smoke told the man. "So I can understand why you came after me. But you were wrong. I'll let you live. But stay with mining. If I ever see you again, I'll kill you."

The young man turned, putting his back to the dead and bloody. He walked slowly up the street, his high-heeled Spanish riding boots pocking the air with dusty puddles.

"Cool, ain't he, Frenchy?" Preacher said.

"Yes," Gaultier said. "Too much so, perhaps. I wonder if killing the men who killed his father will then bring him happiness?"

"I don't know," Preacher replied. "I just wish to hell he'd find him a good woman and settle down."

"He will never settle down," the Frenchman said. "He might try, but he will always drift—like smoke."

"This here is your show, Smoke," Preacher said, as they rode away from the hot spring. "So you call the tune."

"La Plaza de los Leones. That's the closest name on

the list."

"I been there. Reckon it's changed some, though."

"We'll soon see."

"Wanna answer me a question, Smoke?"

"Have I ever held back from you?"

"Reckon not. But you know I helt you back from doin' this for two years, don't you?"

"You didn't hold me back, you just didn't encourage me."

"All right. Have it your way. How come you made up your mind sudden like?"

"Because it was time, Preacher."

That hard flash of precognition again swept over the mountain man. "Son, have you taken a real clost look at the names on that paper? Now, I can't read airy one, but Frenchy read 'em to me. Them people is scattered over three states and territories. Chances of you finding them all is slim, at best."

"I'll find them."

Preacher nodded. "Well, I'll just tag along—keep you away from bad whiskey and bad wimmin. Both of 'em'll kill a body."

"Preacher? I've never known a woman—the way a man should know one."

"Well, your time'll come, Smoke. You'll fall in love one of these days—it happens to the best of us. Then you'll be walkin' into boulders and pickin' flowers and fallin' off your horse."

Smoke grinned. "Did you do that, Preacher?"

"Yep. For a squaw once. I guess I were in love—don't rightly know much 'bout it."

"What happened to her?"

"She died. And I just don't wanna say no more

'bout it."

La Plaza de los Leones, Square of the Lions, was only a few years away from being renamed Walsenburg. Built on the banks of the Cuchara River, the town, by 1869, was already a ranching and farming community with a city government. It was a hundred and fifty miles from the springs to La Plaza, but Smoke's reputation had preceded him.

The city marshall met them just outside of town, having been warned they were on their way.

"Just pull 'em up right there, boys," he told them. "I'm Marshall Crowell. If you boys are lookin' for trouble, then just keep on ridin'."

"There won't be any trouble in your town," Smoke assured. "I'm looking for a man named Casey."

"What do you want with him?"

"That's my business," Smoke said quietly.

"I'm the law." Crowell met the young man's eyes. "And I'm sayin' it's my business."

"Right," Preacher cut in. "You be the city marshall, shore 'nuff. But you ain't the sheriff. Matter of fact, you ain't nothin' outside of the town limits."

Crowell kept his temper. He knew the old man was right. Crowell was western born and reared, and he knew that here, unlike the East he had only read about, a man killed his own snakes, broke his own horses, and settled his affairs his way, without much interference from the law—to date.

"Start trouble in this town, young man," he warned Smoke, "and you'll answer to me."

"Casey," Smoke repeated. "Where is he?"

Crowell hesitated for a few seconds. "His ranch is southeast of here, on the flats. You'll cross a little creek 'fore you see the house. He's got eight hands. They all look like gunnies."

"You got an undertaker in this town?" Smoke asked.

"Sure. Why?"

"Tell him to dust off his boxes—he's about to get some business."

Crowell sat his horse and watched the pair until they were out of sight. He knew about Preacher, for Preacher was a living legend in Colorado when Crowell was still a boy. As much a legend as Carson, Purcell, Williams, or Charbonneau, son of Sacagawea. The young man with him—or was Preacher with the young man?—was rumored to be the fastest gun anywhere in the state.

A horse coming behind him broke the marshall's thoughts. "Tom?" A man's voice.

Crowell turned to look at the shopkeeper.

"You were deep in thought. Trouble?"

"Not for us, I hope."

"Who were those men?"

"One was the old curly wolf, Preacher. The other was the young gun-hand, Smoke."

"Here! Lord, Tom, who are they after?"

"He asked for Casey."

"Lord! Casey owes me sixty-five dollars."

Ten miles out of town, the pair met two hands riding easy, heading into town. Smoke and Preacher sat their saddles in the middle of the range and waited.

"You boys is on TC range," one of the riders informed them, his voice holding none of the famed western hospitality. "So get the hell off. The boss don't like strangers and neither do I."

Smoke smiled. "You boys been ridin' for the brand long?" he asked congenially.

"You deef?" the second rider asked. "We just told you to get!"

"You answer my question and then maybe we'll leave."

"Since '66, when we pushed the cattle up here from Texas—if it's any of your damned business. Now git!"

"Who owns the TC?"

"Ted Casey. Boy, are you crazy or just stupid?"

"My Pa knew a Ted Casey. Fought in the war with him, for the Gray."

"Oh? What be your name?"

"Some people call me Smoke." He smiled. "Jensen."

Recognition flared in the eyes of the riders. They grabbed for their guns but they were far too slow. Smoke's left hand .36 belched flame and black smoke as Preacher fired his Henry one-handed. Horses reared and screamed and bucked at the noise, and the TC riders were dropped from their saddles, dead and dying.

The one TC rider alive pulled himself up on one elbow. Blood poured through two chest wounds, the blood pink and frothy, one .36 ball passing through both lungs, taking the rider as he turned in the saddle.

"Heard you was comin'," he gasped. "You quick, no doubt 'bout that. Your brother was easy." He smiled a bloody smile. "Potter shot him low in the back; took him a long time to die." The rider closed his eyes and fell back to the ground.

"Let's go clean out the rest of nest of snakes," Smoke said.

"There may be men at the ranch didn't have nothin' to do with your Pa and your brother dyin'."

"Yes. I have thought about that. I would say they have a small problem."

"Figured you'd say that, too."

"He that lies with the dogs, riseth with fleas," Smoke said with a smile.

"Huh?"

"It was in one of those books I read at the cabin on the Fork."

"Shoulda burned them gawddamned things. I knowed it all along."

Stopping in a stand of timber a couple of hundred yards from the ranch house, Preacher said, "There she is. Got any plans?"

"Start shooting."

"The house and out-buildin's?"

"Burn them to the ground."

"You a hard youngun, Smoke."

"I suppose I am." He smiled at Preacher. "But I had a good teacher, didn't I?"

"The best around," the mountain man replied.

The house and bunk house was built of logs, with sod roofs. Burn easy, Smoke thought. He yelled, "Casey! Get out here."

"Who are you?" a shout came from the house.

"Smoke Jensen."

A rifle bullet wanged through the trees. High.

"Lousy shot," Preacher muttered.

The rifle cracked again, the slug humming closer.

"They might git lucky and hit one of the horses," Preacher said.

"You tuck them in that ravine over there," Smoke said, dismounting. "I think I'll ease around to the back."

Preacher slid off his mustang. "I'll stay here and worry 'em some. You be careful now."

"Don't worry."

"'Course not," the old man replied sarcastically. "Why in the world would I do that?" He glanced up at the sky. "Seven, maybe eight hours till dark."

"We'll be through before then." Smoke slipped into an arroyo that half circled the house, ending at the rear of the ranch house.

Fifty yards behind the house, he found cover in a small clump of trees and settled down to pick his targets.

A man got careless inside the house and offered part of his forearm on a sill. Smoke shattered it with one round from his Henry. In front of the house, Preacher found a target and cut loose with his Henry. From the screams of pain drifting to Smoke, someone had been hard hit.

"You hands!" Smoke called. "You sure you want to die for Casey? A couple of your buddies already bought it a few miles back. One of them wearing a black shirt."

Silence for a few seconds. "Your Daddy ride with Mosby?" a voice yelled from the house.

"That's right."

"Your brother named Luke?"

"Yeah. He was shot in the back and the gold he was guarding stolen."

"Potter shot him—not me! You got no call to do this. Ride on out and forgit it."

Smoke's reply to that was to put several rounds of .44s through the windows of the house.

Wild cursing came from the house.

"Jensen? The name is Barry. I come from Nevada. Dint have nothin' to do with no war. Never been no further east than the Ladder in Kansas. Nuther feller here is the same as me. We herd cattle; don't git no fightin' wages. You let us ride out?"

"Get your horses and ride on out!" Smoke called.

Barry and his partner made it to the center of the backyard before they were shot in the back by someone in the ranch house. One of them died hard, screaming his life away in the dust of southeast Colorado.

"Nice folks in there," Preacher muttered.

Smoke followed the arroyo until the bunkhouse was between him and the main house. In a pile behind the bunkhouse, he found sticks and rags; in the bunkhouse, a jar of coal oil. He tied the rags around a stake, soaked it in coal oil, lighted it, then tossed it onto the roof of the ranch house. He waited, Henry at the ready, watching the house slowly catch on fire.

Shouts and hard coughing came from inside the ranch house as the logs caught and smoldered, the rooms filling with fumes. One man broke from the cabin and Preacher cut him down in the front yard. Another raced from the back door and Smoke doubled him over with a .44 slug in the guts.

Only one man appeared to still be shooting from the house. Two on the range, at least two hit in the house, and two in the yard. That didn't add up to eight, but maybe, Smoke thought, they had hit more in the house than they thought.

"All right, Casey," he shouted over the crackling of burning wood. "Burn to death, shot, or hung—it's up to you."

Casey waited until the roof was caving in before he stumbled into the yard, eyes blind from fumes. He fired wildly as he staggered about, hitting nothing except earth and air. When his pistol was empty, Smoke walked up to the man and knocked him down, tying his hands behind him with rawhide.

"What do you figure on doin' with him?" Preacher asked, shoving fresh loads into his Henry.

"I intend to take him just outside of town, by that creek, and hang him."

"I just can't figure where you got that mean streak, boy. Seein' as how you was raised—partly—by a gentle old man like me."

Despite the death he had brought and the destruction wrought, Smoke had to laugh at that. Preacher was known throughout the West as one of the most dangerous men ever to roam the high country and vast Plains. The mountain man had once spent two years of his life tracking down and killing—one by one—a group of men who had ambushed and killed a friend of his, taking the man's furs.

"'Course you never went on the hunt for anyone?" Smoke asked, dumping the unconscious Casey across a saddled horse, tying the man on.

The house was now engulfed in flames, black smoke

spewing into the endless sky.

"Well . . . mayhaps once or twice. But that was years back. I've mellowed."

"Sure." The young man grinned. Preacher was still as mean as a cornered puma.

By the banks of a little creek, some distance outside the town limits, Smoke dumped the badly frightened Casey on the ground. A crowd had gathered, silent for the most part, watching the young man carefully build a noose.

"I could order you to stop this," Marshall Crowell said. "But I suppose you'd only tell me I have no jurisdiction outside of town."

"Either that or shoot you if you try to interfere," Smoke told him.

"The man has not been tried!"

"Yeah, he has. He admitted to me what he done," Smoke told the marshall.

"Lots of smoke to the southeast," Crowell observed. "'Bout gone now."

"House fire," Preacher said. "Poor feller lost ever'thing."

"Two men in the back of the house," Smoke said. "Shot in the back. Casey and his men did that. One died hard."

"That does not excuse what you're about to do," the marshall said. He looked around him. "Is anybody goin' to help me stop this lynchin'?"

No one stepped forward. Casey spat in the direction of the crowd. He cursed them.

"No matter what you call this," Crowell said, "I still intend to file a report callin' it murder."

"Halp!" Casey hollered.

"Vengeance is mine, sayeth the Lord!" said the local minister. "Lord, hear my prayer for this poor wretch of a man." He began intoning a prayer, his eyes lifted upward.

Casey soiled himself as the noose was slipped around his neck. He tried to twist off the saddle.

The minister prayed.

"That ain't much of a prayer," Preacher opined sourly. "I had you beat hands down when them Injuns was fixin' to skin me on Platte. Put some feelin' in it, man!"

The minister began to shout and sweat, warming up to his task. The crowd swelled; some had brought a portion of their supper with them. A hanging was always an interesting sight to behold. There just wasn't that much to do in small western towns. Some men began betting as to how long it would take Casey to die, if his neck was not broken when his butt left the saddle.

The minister had assembled a small choir, made up of stern-faced matronly ladies. Their voices lifted in ragged harmony to the skies.

"Shall We Gather At The River," they intoned.

"I personally think 'Swing Low' would be more like it," Preacher opined.

"He owes me sixty-five dollars," a merchant said.

"Hell with you!" Casey tried to kick the man.

"I want my money," the merchant said.

"You got anything to say before you go to hell?" Smoke asked him.

Casey screamed at him. "You won't get away with

this. If Potter or Stratton don't git you, Richards will."

"What's he talkin' about?" Marshall Crowell said.

"Casey was with the Gray—same as my Pa and brother. Casey and some others like him waylaid a patrol bringing a load of gold into Georgia. They shot my brother in the back and left him to die."

Crowell met the young man's hard eyes. "That was war."

"It was murder."

"Hurry up!" a man shouted. "My supper's gittin' cold."

"I'll see you hang for this," the marshall promised Smoke.

"You go to hell!" Smoke told him. He slapped the horse on the rump and Casey swung in the cool, late afternoon air.

"I'm notifying the territorial governor of this," Crowell said.

Casey's boot heels drummed a final rhythm.

"Shout, man!" Preacher told the minister. "Sing, sisters!" he urged on the choir.

"What about my sixty-five dollars?" the merchant shouted.

EIGHT

The men rode up the east side of the Wet Mountains, camping near the slopes of Greenhorn Mountain.

"Way I see it, Smoke," Preacher said, "you got some choices. That marshall is gonna see to it a flyer is put out on you for murder."

Smoke said nothing.

"Son, you got nothin' left to prove. I can't believe your Pa would want you kilt for something happened years back."

"I won't change my name, I won't hide out, and I won't run," Smoke said. "I aim to see this thing through and finished."

"Or get finished," Preacher said glumly.

"Yes."

"Well?"

"I head to Canon City."

"*We* head to Canon City," Preacher corrected.

"All right."

"Been there a time or two." Preacher had been *everywhere* in the West at least a time or two. "Son?

You ain't gonna ride in there and hogtie them folk. That town's nigh on sixty year old. They got a hard man for a sheriff."

"But Ackerman's there."

"That's the one betrayed your brother? The one Luke thought was his friend?"

"That's him."

"Man like that needs killin'."

"That is exactly what I intend to do."

"Figured you'd say that."

A few miles outside of Florence, two riders stopped the pair early one morning. They were rough-looking men, with tied-down guns, the butts worn smooth from much handling. Their Missouri cavalry hats were pulled low, faces unshaven.

"Been waitin' here for you," one said. "Word of you hangin' Casey spread fast. They be warrants out on you 'fore long. You made that marshall look like a fool."

"What's your interest in this?" Smoke asked.

"I rode for the Gray. Know the story of what happened from a man that was there. What we wantin' to tell you is this: One of them hands that was on the range back at the TC beat it quicklike to Canon City. Seen him ride in, horse all lathered up and wind-broke. He ruined a good animal. Went straight to Ackerman's spread, few miles out of town, east. They waitin' for both of you."

"Much obliged to you," Smoke said. "Where you heading?"

"Back to Missouri. Got word that Dingus and Buck

needin' some boys to ride with 'em. Thought we'd give it a whirl. You shore look familiar in the face to me. We met?"

"You was with Bloody Bill the night Jesse gave me this Colt. Tell him hello for me."

"Done. You boys ride easy and ready, now. See you." The outlaws wheeled their horses and were gone, heading east, to Missouri—and into disputed history.

"Now what?" Preacher asked his young partner.

"We'll just ride in for a look-see."

"Figured you'd say that."

"Welcome to Oreodelphia," Preacher said, as they approached Canon City from the south. They stopped, looking over the town.

"Oreo . . . what?"

"Oreodelphia. That's what one feller wanted to name this place—'bout ten year ago. Miners said they couldn't say the damned word, much less spell it. Never did catch on."

"Gold around here?"

"Right smart. Never got the fever myself. Found some nuggets once—threw 'em back in the crick and never told no one 'bout it."

"You may have found a fortune, Preacher."

"Mayhaps, son. But what is it I need that there gold for? Got ever'thing a body could want; couldn't tote no more. I got buckskins to cover me, a good horse, good guns, and a good friend. Had me a right purty watch once, but I had to give 'er up."

"Why?"

"One time a bunch of Cheyennes on the warpath come close to where I was hidin' out in a ravine. I plumb forgot that there watch chimed on the hour. Liked to have done me in. Thought I was dead for shore. Them Injuns was so took with that watch, they forgot 'bout me. I took off a-hightailin'." He laughed. "I bet them Injuns was mad when that watch run down and wouldn't chime no more."

They urged their horses forward. "One more thing I think you should know, Smoke."

"What's that?"

"I hear tell the state's gonna build a brand new prison just outside of town. They might be lookin' to fill it up."

The old mountain man and the handsome young gunfighter rode slowly down the main street of Canon City. They drew some attention, for they were dressed in buckskins and carried their Henry repeating rifles across their saddles, instead of in a boot. And the sheriff and one of his deputies were among those watching the pair as they reined up in front of the saloon and stepped out of the saddle.

Boot heels clumped on the boardwalk as the sheriff walked toward them. Neither Smoke nor Preacher looked up, but both were aware of his approach, and of the fact that a deputy had stationed himself across the street, a rifle cradled in his arms.

"Howdy, boys," the sheriff greeted them.

He received a nod.

The sheriff looked at their horses. "Been travelin', I see."

"A piece," Preacher said.

The sheriff recognized him. "You're the Preacher."

"That's what I'm called."

"And you're the gun-hand called Smoke."

"That's what I'm called."

"You boys plannin' on stayin' long?"

Smoke turned his dark eyes on the sheriff and let them smolder for a few seconds. "Long enough."

The sheriff had seen more than his share of violence; he had seen more shootings, knifings, and hangings than he cared to remember. He had known, and known personally, men of violence: Clay Allison, Wild Bill, and others who were just as mean—or meaner—but never gained the reputation. But something in this young man's eyes made the sheriff back up a step, something he had never done before. And he silently cursed that one step.

"I heard what happened to Casey," the sheriff spoke in low tones. "Nothing like that is going to happen in this town. Don't start trouble here."

Smoke suddenly smiled boyishly and disarmingly. "You don't mind if we buy some supplies, have a few hot meals, and rest for a day or two, do you, sheriff? Take a hot bath?"

"Speak for yourself on that last part," Preacher said.

"Confine yourselves to doing that," the sheriff said, then brushed past the men.

"That lawman's salty, Smoke," Preacher observed correctly.

"But he backed up," the young man replied.

"Yep. They's something 'bout you that'll make a smart man get away from you. And that worries me, some."

"Why?"

"Might mean I ain't too smart."

They stabled their horses and told the stable boy to rub them down and give them grain. They went across the street to a small cafe and had steak, boiled potatoes, and apple pie for twenty five cents apiece.

"These prices," Preacher opined, "this feller'll be retired in a month."

As if by magic, the cafe had emptied of customers with the arrival of the buckskin-clad men. But when the regular diners—who, Smoke observed, ate for fifteen cents each—saw the pair meant no harm, the cafe once more filled with diners.

"Coffee's weak," Preacher bitched, as he sucked at his fourth cup.

"Any coffee that won't float a horseshoe," Smoke said grinning at him, "you'd claim was weak."

"True. What's your plan this time?"

"Check in at the hotel, then get some chairs and sit out front, watch the people pass by."

"Wait for them to come to us, eh?"

"That's right."

"And ifn they force our hand, the sheriff can't bring no charges agin us for defendin' ourselves."

"That is correct."

Preacher ordered another piece of apple pie and another cup of coffee. "To be so young, Smoke, you shore got a sneaky streak in you."

"It's the company I've been keeping for the past four years."

"Might have something to do with it, I reckon."

For two days Smoke and Preacher waited and

relaxed in town, causing no trouble, keeping to themselves. Smoke bathed twice behind the barber shop, and Preacher told him ifn he didn't stop that he was gonna come down with some dreadful illness.

The mountain man and the gunfighter were civil to the men, polite to the ladies. Some of the ladies batted their eyes and swished their bustled fannies as they passed by Smoke.

"You boys sure takin' your time buyin' supplies," the sheriff noted on the second day.

"We like to think things through 'fore buyin'," Preacher told him. "Smoke here is a right cautious man with a greenback. Might even call him tight."

The sheriff didn't find that amusing. "You boys wouldn't be waiting for Ackerman to make a move, would you?"

"Ackerman?" Smoke looked at the sheriff. "What is an Ackerman?"

The sheriff's smile was grim. "What do you boys do for a livin'? I got a law on the books about vagrants."

"I'm retired," Preacher told him. "Enjoyin' the sunset of my years. Smoke here, he runs a string of horses on his ranch up to Brown's Hole."

"You're a long way from Brown's Hole."

"Right smart piece for shore."

"I ought to run you both out of this town."

"Why?" Smoke asked. "On what charge? We haven't caused you any trouble."

"Yet." The sheriff's back was stiff with anger as he strode away. The man knew a setup when he saw one, and this was a setup.

But his feelings were mixed. He owed Ackerman and his bunch of rowdies nothing—they were all troublemakers. Ackerman swung no wide political loop in this country. And there were persistent rumors that Ackerman had been a thief and a murderer during the war—and a deserter. And the sheriff could not abide a coward.

But, he sighed, if he was reading this young man called Smoke right, Ackerman's future looked very bleak.

A hard-ridden horse hammered the street into dust. A hand from the Bar-X slid to a halt. "Ackerman and his bunch are ridin' in, sheriff," the cowhand panted. "They're huntin' bear. Told me to tell you he's gonna kill this kid called Smoke—and anyone else that got in his way."

The sheriff's smile was grudgingly filled with admiration. The kid's patience had paid off. Ackerman had made his boast and his threat; anything the kid did now could only be called self-defense.

The sheriff thanked the cowboy and told him to hunt a hole. He crossed the street and told his deputy to clear the street in front of the hotel.

In five minutes, the main street resembled a ghost town, with a yellow dog the only living thing that had not cleared out. Behind curtains, closed doors, and shuttered windows, men and women watched and waited, ears atune, anticipating the roar of gunfire from the street.

At the edge of town, Ackerman, a bull of a man, with small, mean eyes and a cruel slit for a mouth, slowed his horse to a walk. Ackerman and his hands rode down the street, six abreast.

Preacher and Smoke were on their feet. Preacher stuffed his mouth full of chewing tobacco. Both men had slipped the thongs from the hammers of their Colts. Preacher wore two Colts, .44s. One in a holster, the other stuck behind his belt. Mountain man and young gunfighter stood six feet apart on the boardwalk.

The sheriff closed his office door and walked into the empty cell area. He sat down and began a game of checkers with his deputy.

Ackerman and his men wheeled their horses to face the men on the boardwalk. "I hear tell you boys is lookin' for me. If so, here I am."

"News to me," Smoke said. "What's your name?"

"You know who I am, kid. Ackerman."

"Oh, yeah!" Smoke grinned. "You're the man who helped kill my brother by shooting him in the back. Then you stole the gold he was guarding."

Inside the hotel, pressed against the wall, the desk clerk listened intently, his mouth open in anticipation of gunfire.

"You're a liar. I didn't shoot your brother; that was Potter and his bunch."

"You stood and watched it. Then you stole the gold."

"It was war, kid."

"But you were on the same side," Smoke said. "So that not only makes you a killer, it makes you a traitor and a coward."

"I'll kill you for sayin' that!"

"You'll burn in hell a long time before I'm dead," Smoke told him.

Ackerman grabbed for his pistol. The street exploded in gunfire and black powder fumes. Horses screamed and bucked in fear. One rider was thrown to the dust by his lunging mustang. Smoke took the men on the left, Preacher the men on the right side. The battle lasted no more than ten to twelve seconds. When the noise and the gunsmoke cleared, five men lay in the street, two of them dead. Two more would die from their wounds. One was shot in the side—he would live. Ackerman had been shot three times: once in the belly, once in the chest, and one ball had taken him in the side of the face as the muzzle of the .36 had lifted with each blast. Still Ackerman sat his saddle, dead. The big man finally leaned to one side and toppled from his horse, one boot hung in the stirrup. The horse shied, then began walking down the dusty street, dragging Ackerman, leaving a bloody trail.

"I heard it all!" the excited desk clerk ran out the door. "You were in the right, Mr. Smoke. Yes, sir. Right all the way. Why . . . !" He looked at Smoke. "You've been wounded, sir."

A slug had nicked the young man on the cheek, another had punched a hole in the fleshy part of his left arm, high up. They were both minor wounds. Preacher had been grazed on the leg and a ricocheting slug had sent splinters into his face.

Preacher spat into the street. "Damn near swallered my chaw."

"I never seen a draw that fast," a man spoke from his store front. "It was a blur."

The sheriff and a deputy came out of the jail, walking down the bloody, dusty street. Both men carried Greeners: double-barreled twelve gauge shotguns.

"Right down this street," the sheriff said pointing, "is the doctor's office. Get yourselves patched up and then get out of town. You have one hour."

"Sheriff, it was a fair fight," the desk clerk said. "I

seen it."

The sheriff never took his eyes off Smoke. "One hour," he repeated.

"We'll be gone." Smoke wiped a smear of blood from his cheek.

Townspeople began hauling the bodies off. The local photographer set up his cumbersome equipment and began popping flash-powder, sealing the gruesomeness for posterity. He also took a picture of Smoke.

The editor of the paper walked up to stand by the sheriff. He watched the old man and the young gunhand walk down the street. He truly had seen it all. The old man had killed one man, wounded another. The young man had killed four men, as calmly as picking his teeth.

"What's that young man's name?"

"Smoke Jensen. But he's a devil."

NINE

There was a chill to the air when Smoke kicked off his blankets and rose to add twigs to the still smoldering coals. They were camped along the Arkansas, near Twin Lakes.

"Cold," Preacher complained, crawling out of his buffalo robe. "Can't be far from Leadville."

"How do you figure that?" Smoke asked, slicing bacon into a pan and dumping a handful of coffee into the pot.

"Coldest damn town in the whole country." Preacher put on his hat then tugged on his boots. "I've knowed it to snow on the Fourth of July. So damned cold ifn a man dies in the winter, best thing to do is jist prop him up in a corner for the season. Ifn you wanna bury him, you gotta use dynamite to blast a hole in the ground. Tain't worth the bother. And I ain't lyin', neither."

Smoke grinned and said nothing. He had long since ceased questioning the mountain man's statements; upon investigation, they all proved out.

"Them names on the list, Smoke. Anymore of 'em

in Colorado?"

"Only one more, but we'll let him be. He's in the army up at Camp Collins. An officer. Took the name of a dead man who was killed in the first days of the war. I can't fight the whole Yankee army."

"We goin' back to the Hole?"

"For the time being."

"Good. We'll winter there. Stop along the way and pack in some grub."

Major Powell and his detachment were gone when Preacher and Smoke reached the Hole in mid-September. Two horses were missing from the herd, and the money for them was in the cave. The soldiers had tended to the gardens, eating well from them. Emmett Jensen's grave had been looked after. But the flowers were dying. Winter was not far off.

The two men set about making the cabin snug against the winds that would soon howl cold through the canyon, roaring out of Wyoming, sighing off Diamond Peak. Preacher did a little trapping, for all the good it did him, and for awhile, the man called Smoke seemed to be at peace with himself.

Preacher was surprised and embarrassed that Christmas morning to find a present for him when he awakened. He opened the box and aahed at the chiming railroad watch with a heavy gold fob.

"That little watch and clock shop in Oreodelphia," Preacher recalled. "Seen you goin' in there." He was suddenly ill at ease. "But I dint get nothin' for you."

"You've been giving me presents for years, Preacher.

You've taught me the wilderness and how to survive. Just being with you has been the greatest present of my life."

Preacher looked at him. "Oh, hush up. You plumb sickenin' when you try to be nice." He wound the watch. "Reckon what time it is." He turned his head so Smoke could not see the tears in his eyes.

Smoke glanced outside. "'bout seven, I reckon."

"That's clost enough." He set the watch and smiled as it chimed. "Purty. Best present I ever had."

"Oh, hush up." Smoke smiled. "You plumb sickenin' when you try to be nice."

The winter wore on slowly in its cold, often white harshness. In the cabin, Preacher would sometimes sit and watch Smoke as he read and reread the few books in his possession, educating himself. He especially enjoyed the works of Shakespeare and Burns.

And sometimes he would look at the paper from his father and from Gaultier. And Preacher knew in his heart, whether the young man would admit it or not, he would never rest until he had crossed out all the names.

In the early spring of '70, as the flowers struggled valiantly to push their colors to the warmth of the sun, Smoke began gathering his gear. Wordlessly, Preacher did the same.

"Where we goin' in such an all-fired hurry?" he asked Smoke.

"I've heard you talk about the southwest part of this territory. You said it was pretty and lonely."

"'Tis."

"You know it well?"

"I know the Delores, and the country thereabouts."

"Many people?"

"Not to speak of."

"Be a good place to set up ranching, wouldn't it?"

"Ifn a man could keep his hair. That where we goin'?"

"What is there to keep us here?"

"Nothing a-tall."

Pushing the herd of half-broken mustangs and Appaloosa, the two men headed south into the wild country, populated mainly by Ute, but with a scattering of Navajo and Piute. They crossed the Colorado River just east of what would later become Grand Junction, then cut southeast, keeping west of the Uncompahgre Plateau. Out of Unaweep Canyon, only a few miles from the Delores River, they began to smell the first bitter whiffs as the wind changed.

Preacher brought them to a halt. While Smoke bunched the horses, Preacher stood up in his stirrups to sniff the air. "They's more to it than wood. Sniff the air, son, tell me what you smell."

Smoke tried to identify the mixture of strange odors. Finally he said, "Leather. And cloth. And . . . something else I can't figure out."

Preacher's reply was grim. "I can. Burnin' hair and flesh. You 'bout to come up on what an Injun leaves behind after an attack." He pointed. "We'll put the horses in that box canyon over yonder, then we'll go take a look-see."

Securing the open end of the canyon with brush and rope, the men rode slowly and carefully toward the smell of charred flesh, the odor becoming thicker as they rode. At the base of a small hill, they left their horses and crawled up to the crest, looking down at the horror below.

Tied by his ankles from a limb, head down over a small fire, a naked man trembled in the last moments of life. His head and face and shoulders were blackened cooked meat. The mutilated bodies of other men lay dead. One was tied to the wheel of the burned wagon. He had been tortured. All had died hard.

"You said you heared gunfire 'bout two hours ago," Preacher whispered. "You was right. Gawdamned 'Pache trick, that yonder is. They come up this far ever' now and then, raidin' the Utes."

"How did they get a wagon this far?" Smoke asked.

"Sheer stubbornness. But I hope they weren't no wimmin with 'em. If so, Gawd help 'em."

The men waited for more than an hour, moving only when necessary, talking in low tones.

Finally, Preacher stirred. "They gone. Let's go down and prowl some, give the people a Christian burial. Say a word or two." He spat on the ground. "Gawddamned heathens."

Smoke found a shovel, handle intact, on the ground beside the charred wagon. He dug a long, shallow grave, burying the remains of the men in one common grave, covering the mound with rocks to keep wolves and coyotes from digging up the bodies and eating them.

Preacher walked the area, cutting sign, trying to determine if anyone got away. Smoke rummaged through what was left of the wagon. He found what he didn't want to find.

"Preacher!"

The mountain man turned. Smoke held up a dress he'd found in a trunk, then another dress, smaller than the first.

Preacher shook his shaggy head as he walked. "Gawd have mercy on they souls," he said, fingering the gingham. "Man's a damned fool bringin' wimmin-folk out here."

"Maybe one of them got away?" Smoke said hopefully.

"Tain't likely. But we got to look."

Almost on the verge of giving up after an hour's searching, Smoke made one more sweep of the area. Then he saw the faint shoeprints, mixed in with moccasin tracks. The prints were small; a child, or a woman.

"Good Lord!" Preacher said. "Mayhaps she got clear and run away." He circled the tracks until he got them separated. "Don't see none followin' her. Get the horses, son. We got to find her 'fore dark."

It did not take them long to track her. She was hiding behind some brush, at the mouth of a canyon. Movement of the brush gave her away.

"Girl," Preacher said, "you come on out, now. You 'mong friends."

Weeping was the only reply from behind the brush. Smoke could see one high-top button shoe. A dainty shoe.

"We're not going to hurt you," he said.

More weeping.

"They's a snake crawlin' in there with you," Preacher lied.

A young woman bolted from behind the brush as if propelled from a cannon barrel, straight into the arms of Smoke. With all her softness pressing against him, she lifted her head and looked at him through eyes of light blue, a heart-shaped face framed with hair the color of wheat. They stood for several long heartbeats, gazing at each other, neither of them speaking.

Preacher snorted. "This ain't no place for romance. Come on. Let's get the hell out of here."

Preacher griped and groused, but the young woman insisted upon returning to where the members of her family were buried. She stood for a few moments, looking down at the long, narrow grave.

"My aunt?" she questioned.

"Looks like the savages took her," Preacher said.

"What will they do to her?"

"Depends a lot on her. Was she a looker?"

"I beg your pardon?"

"Was she a handsome woman?"

"She was beautiful."

Preacher shrugged. "Then they'll probably keep her." He did not tell the young woman her aunt might have been—by now—raped repeatedly and then tortured to death. "They'll work her hard, beat her some, but she'll most probably be all right. Some buck with no squaw will bed her down. Then agin, they might trade her off for a horse or rifle."

"Or they might kill her?" she said.

"Yep."

"You don't believe I'll ever see her again, do you?"

"No, Missy, I don't. It just ain't likely. Down in Arizony Territory, back 'bout '51 or '52, I think it was, the Oatman family tried to cross the desert alone. The Yavapais kilt the parents and took the kids. A boy and two gals. The boy run off, one of the gals died. But Olive Oatman lived as a slave with the Injuns for years. They tattooed her chin 'fore she was finally traded off for goods. It's bes' to put your aunty out of your mind. I seen lots of white wimmin lived with Injuns for years; too ashamed to come back to they own kind even ifn they could."

The young woman was silent.

"What's your name?" Smoke asked.

"Nicole," she said, then put her face in her small hands and began to weep. "I don't know what to do. I don't have any family to go back to. I don't have anyone."

Smoke put his arms around her. "Yes, you do, Nicole. You have us."

"Just call me Uncle Preacher," the mountain man said. "Plumb disgustin'."

Smoke rummaged around the still smouldering wagon, looking for any of Nicole's clothing that might have escaped the flames. He found a few garments, including a lace-up corset, which she quickly snatched, red-faced, from him. He also found a saddle that had suffered only minor damage. Everything else was lost.

"Now, how you figure she's a-gonna sit that there

saddle?" Preacher demanded. "What with all them skirts and petti-things underneath?"

"She's not. She found a pair of men's trousers that belonged to her uncle. She can ride astraddle."

"That ain't fittin' for no decent woman. Ain't nobody 'ceptin' a whoore'd do that!"

"What the hell'd you wanna do? Build a travois and drag her?"

Preacher walked away, muttering to himself.

Nicole came to Smoke's side. "I can sit a saddle. I rode as a child in Illinois."

"Is that where you're from?"

"No. I'm from Boston. After my parents died, when I was just a little girl, I came to Illinois to live with my uncle and aunt. What's your name?"

"Smoke. That's Preacher." He jerked his thumb.

She smiled. She was beautiful. "Just Smoke?"

"That's what I'm called."

"At a trading post, we heard talk of a gunfighter called Smoke. Is that you?"

"I guess so."

"They said you'd killed fifty men." There was no fear in her eyes as she said it.

Smoke laughed. "Hardly. A half dozen white men, maybe. But they were fair fights."

"You don't look like a gunfighter."

"What does a gunfighter look like?"

She smiled, white even teeth flashing against the tan of her face.

"Carryin' on like children at a box social," Preacher muttered.

* * *

Nicole went behind a boulder to change out of her tattered and dusty dress. Preacher walked up to his young protégé.

"What are you aimin' to do with her?"

"Take her with us. We sure can't leave her out here."

"Well, hell! I know all that. I mean in the long run. Nearest town's more'un a hundred miles off."

"Well, I . . . don't know."

The mountain man's eyes sparkled. "Ah," he said. "Now I get it. Got your juices up and runnin', eh?"

Smoke stiffened. "I have not given that any thought."

Preacher laughed. "You can go to hell for tellin' lies, boy." He walked off, chuckling, talking to himself. "Yes, siree," he called, "young Smoke's got hisself a gal. Right purty little thing, too. Whoa, boy!" He did a little jig and slapped his buckskin-clad knee. "Them blankets gonna be hotter than a buffalo hunter's rifle after a shoot." He cackled as he danced off, spry as a youngster.

Smoke's face reddened. What the young man knew about females could be placed in a shot glass and still have room for a good drink of whiskey.

"What is Preacher so happy about?" Nicole asked, walking up behind him.

Smoke turned and swallowed hard. Luckily, he did not have a chew of tobacco in his mouth. The men's trousers fitted the woman snugly—very snugly. The plaid man's shirt she now wore was unbuttoned two buttons past the throat, and that was about all the young man could stand.

Smoke lifted his eyes to stare at her face. She was beautiful, her features almost delicate, but with a stubborn set to her chin.

She had freshened up at the little creek and her face wore a scrubbed look.

"Uh . . ." he said.

"Never mind," Nicole said. "I'm sure I know what he was laughing about."

"Ah . . . I've saddled a little mare for you. She's broke, but hasn't been ridden lately. She may kick up her heels a bit."

"Mares do that every now and then," Nicole said coyly, smiling at him.

"Uh . . . yeah! Right."

"Smoke?" She touched his thick forearm, tight with muscle. "I'm not trying to be callous or unfeeling about . . . what happened today. I'm just . . . trying to put it—the bad things—behind me. Out of my mind. Do you understand?"

"Yes." He touched her hand. Soft. "Come on. We'd better get moving."

When Nicole swung into the saddle, the trousers stretched tight across her derriere. Smoke stared—and stared. Then his boot missed the stirrup when he tried to mount and he fell flat on his back in the dust.

"I knowed it!" Preacher said. "Knowed it when I seen 'em a-lookin' at one 'nother. Gawd help us all. He'll be pickin' flowers next. Ifn he can git up off the ground, that is."

The trio pushed the horses and followed the Delores down to its junction with Disappointment Creek. There, they cut slightly west for a few miles, then bore south, toward a huge valley. They would be among the first whites to settle in the valley. Long after Smoke had become a legend, the town of Cortez would spring up, to the south of the SJ Ranch. Midway in the valley, by a stream that rolled gently past a gradually rising knoll, Smoke pulled up.

"Here?" Preacher looked around, approval of the site evident in his eyes. He had taught the young man well.

"Right here," Smoke said. "We'll build the cabin on that small knoll." He pointed. "Afford us the best view in the valley and give us some protection as well. See that spring over there?" he asked Nicole. "It feeds into the creek. Comes out under the knoll. We can dig a well and tap into it, or its source."

"It's so beautiful," she said, looking around her.

"Yep," Preacher teased. "Be a right nice place for a man to start raisin' a family. Shore would."

Smoke blushed and Nicole laughed. She had grown accustomed to the mountain man's teasing, and liked him very much. But it was to the tall young man she more often cast her blue eyes. The thought of him being the much-talked about and feared and hated gun-fighter was amusing to her. Smoke was so gentle and shy.

Nicole had a lot to learn about the West and its men. And she was to learn very quickly and harshly—in the time left her.

TEN

First a house was built, of adobe and logs and rocks, with rough planking and sod for a roof. Smoke would not settle for a dirt floor; instead he carefully smoothed and shaped the logs, which had to be dragged from the forest, which lay to the northeast. The work was hard and backbreaking, but no one complained, except Preacher, who bitched all the time, about almost everything. Neither Smoke nor Nicole paid any attention to him, knowing it was his way and he was not going to change.

Nicole never spoke of leaving, and Smoke never brought it up. Preacher just grinned at them both.

Twice during the summer of '70, the trio came under attack from the Utes, and twice they were beaten back, with the Utes taking heavy losses from the rifles in the fortlike home on the small hill. Nicole, to the surprise of the men, proved not at all reluctant to learn weapons, and became a better than average shot with a rifle. On the final attempt by the Utes to drive the whites from the land, Nicole showed what backbone she had by knocking a brave off his circling pony, wounding him slightly, then calmly finishing him off with another round. Turning from the peephole, she saw two braves attempting to chop their way in through the back door. She killed them both.

The Utes in the huge valley never again attacked the home, choosing instead to live under a wary peace with the two men and the woman they came to call Little Lightning.

But it was with awe in her eyes that Nicole watched Smoke handle his guns: with calmness and cold deliberation. Death at the end of his arms. Even in haste, he never seemed to hurry, choosing his targets, almost never missing, even at the most incredible range.

Arriving too late to plant a garden, Smoke and Preacher hunted for food, drying and curing the meat for the harsh winter that was ahead of them. When the rough house was up, the well dug, close to the house, and food to last them, Preacher saddled his horse one morning and rigged a pack horse.

"Headin' east," he told them. "Over to the Springs, maybe. Mayhaps beyond. They's things we be needin'. Pump for the kitchen; pipe—other things. I'll be back—maybe—'fore the first snow. Ifn I ain't, I ain't comin' back till spring. I may decide to winter in the mountains with some old cronies still up there. Don't know yet. See you younguns later."

He rode off, not looking back, for if he had done that, Smoke and Nicole would have been able to see the twinkle of mischief in the eyes, the eyes full of cunning and knowledge—of a man and woman and a long winter ahead.

Preacher had decided the young folks needed some time to themselves, and he was going to give it to them. He also wanted to test the wind; see if the legend of Smoke had grown any since the shootings of the past summer. He suspected the stories had mushroomed—and he was right.

Nicole touched Smoke's arm. "When will he be back?"

"When he feels like it." Smoke was experiencing a rush of emotions; a sense of loss in the pit of his stomach. This would be the first time in five years he and Preacher would be separated for any length of time. And Smoke knew, although he could never put it into words, he loved the cantankerous old mountain man—loved him as much as he had his own father.

"Why did he leave like that?" Nicole asked. "Without even a fare-thee-well?"

"Lots of reasons." The young man's eyes were on the fast disappearing dot in the valley. "He knows he doesn't have many winters left, and he wants to be alone some—that's the way he's lived all his life. And he wants us to have some time together."

He looked down at the petite woman. She met his gaze.

The wind whistled through the valley, humming around them, touching them, caressing them with a soft, invisible hand, making them more conscious of their being together.

A flush touched her face. "I'll . . . I'd better see to the breakfast dishes."

"I've got to check on the herd," Smoke said, keeping his eyes averted. "Keep a gun close by. I'll be back by midday."

"I'll be waiting for you," she replied, her voice husky.

He again met her gaze, for the first time seeing a fire among the gentle blue. .

It scared the hell out of him.

Smoke spent the morning checking on his herd, looking over the new colts, crisscrossing the valley floor, his eyes alert for any Indian sign. He knew he was stalling, putting off the trip back to the house—and to Nicole. He was not expecting any trouble from the Utes, for when they saw he was not going to be run off the land, and was not—at this time—the forerunner of more whites, they had made gestures of peace toward him, and he had accepted that offer.

Twice he had shared meat he had killed with the Utes. And once he had come upon a young Ute boy who had been badly injured in a fall near Ute Peak. Smoke had spent two lonely nights with the boy, watching over him, tending to his injuries. He had then constructed a travois and carried the boy to his camp.

The years with Preacher had stood Smoke well, for he had slept in countless Indian camps and had learned their ways—as much as any white man could—and Smoke knew sign language, which seemed to be universal among the many tribes.

The next morning he had ridden out of the Indian camp, as safely as he had ridden in. There had been no more trouble from the Utes. But the Ute were not the only tribe in this part of the country; there were Piute, and to the south, Navajo and some Apache. And the Apache were friends to no white man—and damn few other Indians.

In this section of the young nation, if one grew careless, one could get suddenly dead.

He turned Seven's nose north. Toward the cabin. Toward Nicole.

He stabled the Appaloosa, rubbed him down, and forked hay for him. Then Smoke washed at the stream behind the hill.

Nicole was silent as she ladled beans and venison on their plates, then sat down across the rough-hewn table from Smoke. There was unexpected tension between them. They had been alone before, several times, when Preacher was off wandering; but this was different. They were *really* alone.

"How's the stock?" Nicole asked, her eyes fixed on the plate.

"Fine. Two colts growing like weeds. No sign of Apaches. Saw some deer. Didn't think to shoot. We got food enough for a time."

After that, conversation did not lag—it died.

Smoke was aware of his heart thudding heavily in his chest. Nicole was nervous, twice dropping her fork. The meal seemed to be taking a lot longer than usual. Smoke suddenly noticed she had changed her dress since his leaving that morning. She had put on her best dress. Usually she wore men's britches she had tailored to fit her. The dress seemed to bring out her womanhood.

Smoke reached for the honey pot to sweeten his coffee and knocked over the clay jug.

"I'll get it," they spoke in unison, as honey dripped from the table to the floor.

They both rose and bent down, banging their heads together. Smoke put his hand on the edge of the table for support and it toppled over, dumping him to the floor, everything on the table spilling and pouring on his head and all over her.

"Oh—hell!" Nicole said.

That startled Smoke. It was the first time he'd ever heard a lady swear.

They looked at each other: Smoke, with beans and venison on his head; Nicole, with honey and gravy dripping off her chin. They began laughing and pointing at each other.

He offered his hand and she took it, both of them rising to their feet, slipping in the mess on the floor. He took off his shirt and headed for the door.

"Where are you going?" she asked.

"To the creek, to take a bath. I'll holler when it's all clear."

She smiled, and Smoke was not at all sure he liked the look in her eyes.

Standing in the water, with lather from the waist up, Smoke coud not believe his eyes when Nicole appeared on the bank, towels in her hand. He closed his eyes and turned his back, speechless, when she began taking off her stained dress. Then she was by his side.

"Give me the soap," she said. "I'll scrub your back."

"Nicole . . ." he managed to croak.

"Turn around, Smoke—look at me."

He turned, and she laughed when she saw his eyes were tightly closed.

"You'll have to open them sometime," she whispered.

He did.

And there was no more need for words.

* * *

Full dark when he slipped from her side to step out into the coolness of Colorado night. He left Nicole sprawled in sleep in his bed. Smoke rolled a cigarette and lit it, the match explosive in the night. He inhaled deeply.

He felt drained, but yet, ten feet tall. He felt weak, but yet powerful. They had made love, and told each other of their love, for what seemed like hours, on the cool grass of the creek bank. They had bathed and soaped each other, then walked naked back to the house where they made love again. Then they had slept.

In all his young but eventful life, the man called Smoke had never before experienced anything to compare with the sensual events of that afternoon and early evening with Nicole, in the quiet valley.

He stepped back into the house, pulling on his boots and buckling his guns around his lean waist. Shirtless, he stepped back out into the purple night.

He checked the grounds around the house, then the corral and the lean-to that served as a barn. Quiet. It really was an unnecessary move, since Seven would sound an alarm if a stranger approached, but it made Smoke feel better to double check. He went back into the house and stoked up the fire, putting on coffee to boil, the pot hanging on a swivel iron, attached to the fireplace wall. He sensed, rather than heard, Nicole enter the room.

She was barefoot, wearing one of his shirts, and he thought she had never appeared more beautiful.

"Would you like me to fix supper?"

He rose and shook his head. She came into his arms.

"I love you," he said.

Her reply was a loving whisper; a commitment

spoken from the heart.

Preacher did not return that winter of 1870/71, and although Smoke did not admit his feelings aloud, Nicole knew he was worried about the old mountain man, fearing he might be hurt, or dead.

And it was Nicole who finally eased his mind, calming the unrest in him.

"How old is Preacher?" she asked one evening. A steady rain fell in the valley, occasionally mixed with sleet and snow. The winter had been a hard one, requiring brutal work from both of them just to stay alive.

"He's pushin' seventy. Least that's what he'll admit to bein'. Getting old."

"And he's lived a very long, exciting, and fruitful life. He wouldn't want to die in a bed, would he? He'd want to pass this life the way he's lived—in the wilderness. And wouldn't he be sad if he knew you were sad?"

He smiled, his mood lifting from him. He looked at her, something he never tired of doing. "Yes, Nicole, you're right. As usual."

She came to him, sitting very unladylike in his lap, in the wood and rawhide chair, the frame covered with a bearskin. "We've got to get married, Smoke."

"We are. We said we wanted to wait until Preacher came back."

"Well . . . I'm pretty sure we're going to have a baby."

He sat stunned in the chair. "Nicole, we're better than a hundred miles from the nearest doctor."

"I went to nursing school, honey. There is nothing to worry about. All I want is for us to be married. I want the baby to have a legal name."

"Preacher told me there was a little settlement of Mormons just west of here—over in Utah Territory. It'll be a week there and a week back. Can you stand the ride?"

She smiled and kissed him. "Just watch me."

The air was still cool when they rode out of the valley, heading for Utah. But spring was in the air, evident in the leafing trees, the plants, and the flowers that grew wild, coloring the valley. Nicole sat her little mare, Smoke rode Seven.

Nicole looked back at the cabin she had called home for months. "How dangerous is this trip?"

"We might go there and back without seeing an Indian. We might be ambushed ten miles from the cabin. No way to answer that question. I don't know much about Utah Territory, so we'll be seeing it for the first time—together."

They camped on the third night just north of the Hovenweep, near Keely Canyon. They had seen a few Indians on the third day—the first since leaving the valley—Weminuche Ute. But they did not bother the man and woman, but only watched through obsidian eyes, faces impassive. They were armed with ancient rifles and bows and arrows, and perhaps they did not want to risk a fight against the many-shoot rifles of the man and woman; perhaps they did not feel hostile that day; perhaps they were hunting and did not want to take the time for an attack. With an Indian, one never knew.

On the fifth day, Smoke figured they were in Utah Territory—probably had been all day—and the settlement of Mormons should be in sight. But all they found were rotting, tumble-down cabins, and no signs of life.

"Preacher said they were here in '55," Smoke said. "Wonder where they went?"

Nicole's laughter rang out over the deserted collection of falling-down cabins. "Honey, that's sixteen years ago." Her eyes swept the land, spotting an old, weed-filled graveyard. "Let's look over there."

The last faded date on a rotting headmarker was fourteen years old.

In the largest building of the more than a dozen cabins, they found a rusting tin box and pried open the lid. They found rotting papers that crumbled at the touch.

Smoke took Nicole out into the sunlight. "I know what I'll do," he said.

He took a small hammer and a nail from the side pack of his packhorse, carried in case an animal threw a shoe. He built a fire and spent an hour heating and hammering the nail into a crude ring. When it cooled, he slipped it on her third finger, left hand.

"It'll have to do," he said. "Close as I can make us to being really married."

She kissed him and said, "Let's go home."

ELEVEN

Preacher was sitting on the rough bench in front of the cabin when they rode into the yard. He was spitting tobacco juice and whittling on a piece of wood.

"Howdy," he greeted them, as if he had been gone only a day instead of months. "Where you two younguns been?"

"We might ask you the same question," Smoke replied.

"Ramblin'. Seein' God's country in all its glory."

"We got married," Nicole said proudly, showing him her nail ring.

"Right nice," he acknowledged, looking first at the ring, then into her eyes. "You with child, girl?"

She blushed. "Yes, sir."

"Figured ya'll get into mischief while I's gone. Tain't no big deal; I helped birth dozens of papooses in my time. Woman does all the work; man just gets in the way. Who spoke the words?"

"Nobody," Smoke said. "Couldn't find a minister. Went all the way into Utah Territory looking."

"Well . . . I always believed it was what was in your hearts that counted. Knowed you was in love when I seen you fall off your horse."

"I didn't fall off my horse!"

"Did, too."

"Did not!"

"I'll go fix supper," Nicole said.

When she had closed the door to the cabin, Preacher said, "Good thing you didn't ride east, boy—warrants out for you all over the place."

They walked to the lean-to and stabled the horses, rubbing them down with burlap. Preacher gave Smoke the news.

"Got warrants for you with your pitcher on 'em at the Springs and at Walsenburg. Don't ride no further east than the Los Pinos—you hear?"

Smoke looked at him, then opened his mouth to protest.

"You married now, son. You got 'sponsibilities to that there woman who's a-carryin' your child. And you got men huntin' you. That there Potter and Richards . . . 'mong others. Price on your head, too. Big money. They some 'fraid of you, boy—or something like it."

"It's a mystery to me. What'd you hear about Potter and Stratton and Richards?"

"They all up in Ideeho Territory. Up in the wild country. All live in or around a town called Bury."

"B-e-r-r-y?"

"No. Like you plant somebody in the ground. Way I got the story, Smoke, your Pa rode in that there town like a wild man, reins 'tween his teeth, both hands full of Colts. Kilt three or four, wounded two-three more, and took a right smart 'mount of gold them men took from the Rebs. Way I heared it, no one knowed him up there in Bury, so he hung around for a week or two 'fore he made his move, listenin' till he learned where the gold was."

"Wonder what he did with the gold?"

Old eyes studied the young man. "You interested in it?"

"Not in the least."

"I hoped you'd say that."

"If they leave me alone, I'll leave them alone."

"It ain't gonna work thataway, boy."

"What do you mean?"

"You got bounty hunters sniffin' your back trail. They's at least three thousand dollars on your head, dead or alive. All of it put up by them three men up in the territory. That's big money, boy—big money. That's why I come back so soon. Got to have somebody watchin' your back."

"Don't those bounty hunters know the truth about me? About what happened to Pa and Luke?"

"They don't care, son. They after the money and to hell with how they earn it. Most bounty hunters is scum. I'd shoot a bounty hunter on sight—take his hair."

"We're going to raise horses here, Preacher. Run some cattle directly. You and me and Nicole. We're going to raise a family, and our children will need a grandfather—that's you, you old goat."

"Thank you. Nicest thing you've said to me in months."

"I haven't seen you in months!"

"That's right. You keep them guns of yourn loose. When the girl gonna birth?"

"November, she thinks."

"Just like a woman. Don't never know nothin' for sure."

The summer passed uneventfully, with Smoke tending to his huge gardens and looking after his growing herd of horses. Preacher hunted for game, curing some of the meat, making pemmican out of the rest.

In the first week of July, much to Preacher's disgust, Nicole sent him off to the nearest town for some canning jars.

"What the hell is a cannin' jug?"

"Jars," she corrected. "They have screw-down, airtight lids. They keep food fresh and goodtasting for months."

"Well, I'll be damned."

"Probably," Smoke said, saddling Preacher's pony.

"And don't forget the lids," Nicole reminded him. "And the vinegar. "And you come right back, now, Preacher. No dillydallying around, you hear?"

"Yes, ma'am," he said sourly. "And don't fergit the lids!" he mimicked under his breath. "Shore hope none of my compadres see me doin' this. Never live it down."

He continued to mutter as he rode off. "I fit a grizzly bear and won one time," he said. "Now I'm runnin' errands to git jug lids. Ain't nobody got no respect for an old man."

If anyone else had called him an old man, Preacher would have dented his skull with the butt of his Henry.

The nearest town of any size—other than the

Springs, and Preacher could not go there; too many people knew him and might try to track him back to Smoke—was Del Norte, located just a few miles south of the Rio Grande, on the eastern slopes of the San Juan Forest.

He knew of a town being built at the site of old Antoine Robidoux's trading post, up close to the Gunnison, but he doubted they would have any canning jars and lids, so he pointed his pony's nose east-northeast, to avoid settlements as much as possible. He rode through the western part of the San Juan's, cross the Los Pinos, through the Weminuche, then followed the Rio Grande into Del Norte—a long bit of traveling through the wilderness. But Preacher knew all the shortcuts and places to avoid.

As Preacher rode into town, coming in from the opposite direction, deliberately, his eyes swept the street from side to side, settling on a group of men in front of a local saloon. Most were local men, but Preacher spotted two as gun-hands.

He knew one of them: Felter. An ex-army sergeant who had been publicly flogged and dishonorably discharged for desertion in the face of the enemy; the enemy being the Cheyenne up in the north part of the state. But Preacher knew the man was no coward—he just showed uncommon good sense in getting away from a bad situation. After his humiliation and discharge from the army, Felter had turned bounty hunter, selling his gun skills—which were considerable —to the highest bidder. He was an ugly brute of a man, who had killed, so it was said, more than twenty men. He was quick on the draw, but not as quick as Smoke, Preacher knew. Nobody he had ever seen or heard of was that quick. He cut his eyes once more to Felter. The man had been accused of rape—twice.

The other man standing beside Felter looked like Canning, the outlaw. But Preacher was not sure of that. If it was Canning, and he was riding with Felter, they were up to no good—and that was fact.

In a general store, Preacher sized up the shopkeeper as one of those pinch-mouthed Eastern types. Looked like he might be henpecked, too.

Preacher bought a little bit of ribbon for Nicole to wear in her hair, and some pretty gingham for a new dress—she was swellin' up like a pumpkin.

"Got any cannin' jars?"

The shopkeeper nodded. "Just got a shipment of those new type with the screw top. Best around."

"Can you pack 'em for travel over some rough country—headin' east?" Preacher lied.

"I can."

Preacher ordered several cases and paid for them. "Put 'em out back. I'll pick 'em up later on. My old woman is 'bout to wart me plumb to death. Up to her bustle in green beans and sich. Know what I mean? Never should have got hitched up."

"Sir." The shopkeeper leaned forward. "I know *exactly* what you mean. By all that is holy, I do."

"Walter!" A shrill voice cut the hot air of the store. "You hurry up now and bring me my tea. Stop loafing about, gossiping like a fisherwoman. Hurry up!"

Preacher cringed at the thought of being married to someone who sounded like an angry puma with a thorn in its paw. *God!* he thought, *her voice would chip ice.*

"Walter!" the voice squalled from the rear of the store, causing the short hairs on the back of Preacher's

neck to quiver.

Black hatred flashed across the shopkeeper's face.

"Git you a strap," Preacher suggested. "Wear 'er out a time or two."

The man sighed. "I have given that some thought, sir. Believe me, I have."

"Good luck," Preacher told him. He walked out into the street, his Henry cradled in his arms.

A young man in a checkered shirt, a bright red bandanna tied about his neck, dark trousers tucked into polished boots, and wearing two pearl-handled pistols, grinned at the mountain man.

"Hey, grandpa! Ain't you too old to be walkin' around without someone to look after you? You likely to forget your way back to the old folks' home."

The barflies on the porch laughed. All but Felter. He knew the breed of men called mountain man, and knew it was wise to leave them alone, for they had lived violently and usually reacted in kind.

Preacher glanced at the young would-be tough. Without slowing his stride, he savagely drove the butt of his Henry into the loudmouth's stomach. The young smart aleck doubled over, vomiting in the street. Preacher paused long enough to pluck the pistols from leather and drop them in a horse trough.

"You run along home, now, sonny," Preacher told him, over the sounds of retching and the jeering laughter of the loafers on the porch. "Tell your Ma to change your diapers and tuck you into bed. You 'pear to me to need some rest."

Preacher stepped into the dark bar, allowed his eyes to adjust to the sudden gloom, and walked to the counter, ordering whiskey with a beer chaser.

The batwings swung open, boots on the sawdust-covered floor. The marshall. "Trouble out there, old-timer?"

"Nothin' I couldn't handle, young-timer."

The marshall chuckled. "Calls himself Kid Austin. He's been overdue for a comedown for some time. Thinks he's quite a hand with those fancy guns."

Preacher glanced at the lawman. "He'll never make it. They's a lot of salty ol' boys ridin' the hoot-owl trail that'll feed them guns to him. An inch at a time."

The marshall ordered a beer, then waited until the barkeep was out of earshot. He put his elbows on the bar and said softly, "You're the Preacher; man who rides with the young gun, Smoke. Don't talk, just listen. The bounty's been upped on your friend's head. That's the word I get. Someone up in the Idaho Territory is out to get Smoke."

"Potter, Stratton, and Richards."

"That's right. Potter is big . . . politically. Richards is in mining and cattle. Stratton *owns* the town of Bury. Those two gunfighters on the porch, Felter and Canning, work for those three men. They got a bunch of hardcases camped just north of town. When you leave, and I hope it's soon, ride out easy and cover your trail."

"Thanks."

"No need for that. I just know what happened in the war, that's all. Can't abide a traitor."

Preacher glanced at him.

"Since that first shooting, back at the mining camp, the story's spread. I reckon all the way to the Idaho Territory. But there's more. Your friend has a sister named Jane—right?"

"He don't speak none of her."

"Well, she's up in the territory now."

"Let me guess: She's in Bury."

"Yeah. She's Richards's woman. He keeps her."

"I'll tell him."

When Preacher rode out of Del Norte, he did so boldly, not wanting to implicate the shopkeeper, maybe leaving him open to rough treatment from Felter or Canning. Poor fellow had enough woes to contend with from that braying wife. Preacher picked up his jars, secured them well, then rode out to the east.

He didn't think he was fooling anybody, for Felter knew him; knew he was friends with the young gunfighter. He would be followed.

Preacher rode easy, constantly checking his back trail. He rode across the San Luis Valley, slowly edging north. No one alive knew Colorado like the Preacher, and he was going to give his followers a rough ride.

By noon of the second day, Preacher had spotted his trackers. He grinned nastily, then headed his horses toward the Great Sand Dunes. If any of those behind him had any pilgrim in them, this is where Preacher would cut the sheep from the goats.

He skirted the southernmost part of San Luis Creek, filled up his canteens and watered his horses, and grinning, headed for the dunes. On the east side of the lake, Preacher pulled into a stand of timber, carefully smoothed out his trail with brush and sand droppings, then slipped back and waited.

He watched two men, neither of them Felter or Canning, lose his trail and begin to circle. Leaving his horses ground reined, he worked his way to the edge of the timber until he was close enough to hear them talking.

"Damned ol' coot!" one of them said. "Where'd he go?"

"Relax," his partner said. "The boss's got twenty men workin' all around. We got him boxed. He can't get out."

Old coot! Preacher thought. *Your Ma's garters I can't get out!*

"Relax, hell! I want that five thousand dollars."

The ante was going up.

"How much is on the ol' fart's head?"

Old fart! Preacher silently raged.

"Nothin'," the meaner-looking of the pair said with a grin. "It's the gunfighter Richards and them want. That old man ain't worth a buffalo turd."

Buffalo turd! Preacher almost turned purple.

"We'll take the old man alive, make him tell where the kid's at, then kill him."

You just dug your own grave, Preacher thought.

The two men sat their horses. They rolled cigarettes. "How come all this interest in this Smoke? I ain't never got the straight of it."

"Personal, way I heard it. The kid's sister is Richards's private woman up in Bury. I ain't never been there so I can't say if she's a looker. Probably is. Then they's the gold.

"Seems the kid's brother was a Reb in the war, on a patrol bringin' gold in for the South. Richards and them others killed the Rebs and took the gold—'bout a hundred or so thousand dollars of it. 'Bout three-four years back, the kid's Daddy comes a-bustin' into Bury—'fore it was a town proper—and killed some of

Richards's men. Took back some of the gold. 'Bout forty thousand of it, so I heard—but some of it was dust that had been recently washed. Richards thinks the kid has it . . . wants it back and the kid dead."

Preacher grinned. He had thought all along Emmett buried the gold with him. Smart man.

Preacher jacked back the hammer of his Henry and blew both men out of the saddle. "Call me an old fart and a buffalo turd, will you!"

Preacher rode hard to the north, following the creek, going from first one side to the other, many times riding down the middle of the creek to hide his horses' tracks. Just south of the small settlement called Crestone, Preacher headed west, across the valley, undercutting another settlement between the San Luis and the Saguache Creeks. He was out of supplies when he reached Saguache. Picketing his pack animals just outside of town, he rode in, just in time for a hanging.

In the early 1870s, almost every third building in the town was a saloon, and it was a rough and rowdy place. Preacher rode to a general store, got his supplies, and asked who was getting hanged, and for what?

"Some tinhorn gambler named Anderson. Killed a man last night during a card game. Fellow caught him cold-deckin' and braced him. Gambler had one of them little belly guns. Had the trial this mornin'. Judge and jury and all. Lasted forty minutes. Jury deliberated for five minutes. You wanna come watch him swing?"

"Thanks. I best be travelin'. Headin' east," he lied.

"Best be glad you ain't headin' west, lots of hardcases thataway. Lookin' for that outlaw gunfighter and murderer Smoke Jensen. Got six thousand dollars on his head and the ante's goin' up."

"I'm too old for that kind of nonsense," Preacher said. "Leave the hard ridin' and the gunsmoke to the young bucks."

"I know what you mean." The shopkeeper laughed, patting his ample belly. "'Sides, with me it'd be unfair to the horse!"

Outside of town, Preacher swung wide and headed west, into the Cochetopa Hills, then south into the wilderness, then angled southwest, straight through some of the wildest and most beautiful country in the world. Days later, in the Needle Mountains, he was ambushed.

He felt he was being watched as he rode, but figured it was Indians—and Indians didn't worry him, since most of them thought him to be crazy, and he could usually ride through them, singing and cackling.

The slug that almost tore him from the saddle hit him in the left shoulder, driving out his back. Preacher slammed his heels to his pony's side and, keeping low in the saddle, headed for a hole he knew in the mountains. Through his pain, he could hear men yelling off to his right.

"Get him alive! Don't kill him."

But "getting Preacher" took more doing than the men chasing him had. Another rifle barked, the slug hitting him in the leg, deflected off his leg bone and angled upward, ripping a hole when it exited out his hip, taking a piece of bone with it. Savagely reining his pony, Preacher leveled his Henry. He emptied two saddles and shot the horse out from under a third rider, grinning with grim satisfaction as the horse fell on the man, crushing him. The man's screamings ripped through the mountains. Preacher slipped away, hunting a hole where he could tend to his wounds; he was losing a lot of blood.

Preacher rode hard, barely able to see, barely able to hang on to his saddle horn. The pack animals trotted along, keeping pace, frightened. Finally, in desperation, he tied himself in the saddle.

All though the afternoon he rode, half conscious, until he reached a small lake just west of the Animas. There he slid to the ground, dragging his bad leg. In a fog of pain, Preacher loosened the saddle cinch, allowing air to flow between saddle and hide. What he did not need now was a galled-up horse. He was fearful of removing the saddle; didn't know if he would have the strength to swing it back on the pony. He put on his pickets, and collapsed to the earth.

All though the cold night he dreamed of his Indian wives and his kids, as his wounds festered and infected, fevering him. Their images were blurred, and he could not make out their faces.

He dreamed of the mountains and the valleys as they were when he first saw them, close to sixty years back. Lush and green and wild and beautiful. And he dreamed of his compadres, those men who, with Preacher, blazed the trails and danced and sang and whooped and hollered at the rendezvous . . . back when he—and they—were full of piss and vinegar and fire.

But most of them were now dead.

He dreamed of the battles he'd had, both with white and red men. And he wondered if his life, as the way of life of the red man, was ending.

When the chill of dawn touched him with her misty hand, Preacher knew he was close to death.

TWELVE

His babbling and shouting woke him, jerking him into a world filled with pain. "Got to get to Smoke!" he was saying as he opened his eyes. "Got to get to my boy!"

And he knew his feelings toward the tall young man were just as parental as if he were his own flesh and blood.

And he knew he loved the young man with the dark brooding eyes and the cat-quick guns.

Dragging himself to the lake, he washed his wounds and bound them, the sight of them sickening him. He had been hit much harder than this, but that was years back, when he was younger and stronger. He knew he should prepare poultices for his wounds, but didn't know if he had the strength, and, more importantly, the time.

He dragged himself to his pony and tightened the cinch and swung into the saddle. "I'm seventy year old," he muttered. "Lived past my time. Turned into a babblin' ol' fool—maybe I am touched in the head. But I got to warn my boy they's comin'. And I got to cover my tracks better than an Injun."

Having said that, he touched his heels to the pony's side and moved out, gritting his stubs of teeth against the waves of pain that ripped through him.

Modern day doctors would have said what the old man did was impossible for a man half his age. But modern day doctors do not know and will never know the likes of the mountain men who cut the trails of the way west.

A chill was in the morning air when Preacher rode up to the cabin on the knoll in the valley. He was a gaunt shell of the man who had ridden out in the middle of the summer. Through sheer iron will, stubbornness, and hard-headed cantankerousness, he had brought the pack animals with him.

"Howdy, purty thing." He grinned at Nicole. "I brung your durned ol' cannin' jugs." Then he fell from his pony and into the arms of Smoke.

They tended to his wounds, as best they could, for his leg had become infected and it was swollen and grotesque. Nicole turned a tear-stained face to her husband.

"I think he's dying, Smoke."

"Bend down here, son," Preacher said. "I got

something to tell you—and don't argue with me. I ain't time for no debate."

Smoke squatted beside the bed.

"I covered my back trail," Preacher whispered. "So you be safe for a time." Slowly and with much pausing for breath, he told Smoke and Nicole what he knew, and about the gold in the bottom of his father's grave at the Hole.

"When your woman births the baby, wait till spring and then get the hell out of this country. Find you a safe place to live out your lives. Right now, you get my fancy buckskins out of that there trunk over in the corner and then leave me be for a while."

On the porch, Nicole asked, "What is he going to do?"

Smoke sighed heavily, a numbness gripping his heart. "Get all dressed up in his fancy buckskins and sash and such, prepare himself to die, mountain-man style."

Smoke and Nicole sat on the porch of the cabin and waited, listening as Preacher hummed a French song as he dressed.

"I don't know why he's doing this," Nicole said, tears running down her face.

"He's doing it because he's a mountain man." Smoke's eyes were on the mountains in the distance. "I've got to do something." He rose and walked to the lean-to.

He selected a gentle horse, a mare, too old for breeding. He saddled her and took her back to the cabin. Preacher was waiting with Nicole on the porch.

Preacher's eyes touched the horse, returned to

Smoke. "I see you didn't forget ever'thing I learned you."

"No, sir," Smoke said, fighting back tears. "Preacher? What is your Christian name?"

The old man smiled. "Arthur was my first name—why?"

"Because if we have a son, I want to name him after you."

"That'd be right nice. Now help me on that nag yonder and stand back."

Preacher was dressed in clean, beaded buckskins. His dying suit. He wore new leggings and moccasins and a wide red sash around his waist. A cap of skunk hide and hair on his head.

"You look grand," Smoke said.

"You tell lies, too," Preacher retorted. "Help me on the mare."

In the saddle, Preacher looked at Smoke. "You know I'm gonna shoot this horse, don't you, son?"

Smoke nodded. Nicole put her face in her hands and wept. "I don't understand," she said.

"So I can have something to ride when my human body is gone, girl. So don't you fret and carry on. One old life is endin', but you carryin' new life. That's the way of the world." He looked at Smoke. "You be mindful of what I learned you, boy, you hear?"

"Yes, sir."

He rode off without looking back, riding toward the high, far mountains. There, he would select his place to die. He would go out of this world as he had lived in it—alone.

"You know what?" Smoke said to Nicole, as they stood and watched him disappear. "I never even knew his last name."

Autumn touched the valley under the shadows of the great mountains, painting the landscape with a multi-colored brush: the grass a deep tan, the trees golden, the sky blue, and the flowers white and purple and red. On a huge rock by the banks of the creek, Smoke chipped Preacher's name, when he died, and his approximate age. The course of the creek has long since shifted, the bed now part of grazing land, but the huge rock remains. And far in the mountains, high above the West Delores, time and wind have scattered the bones of man and horse. But some locals say that in early fall, on a clear night, if one listens with ears and heart, you can hear the sounds of a slow-moving old mare, carrying a grizzled old mountain man. The old man is singing a French song as he completes his circle, before dismounting to rest for another year, his eyes on a valley far off in the distance.

Of course, that's just a myth. A local legend. Folklore. Certainly isn't *real.* But in the 1930s when the CCC boys were working in the valley, they tried to move the huge boulder with four names chipped deep into it. Something frightened them so badly none of them would ever again go near the boulder. Work was halted at the site.

The local rancher would only say, "I told you so."

And some say Preacher did not die of his wounds, but lay near death in an Indian village for months, while one of his daughters took care of him. Some say the old man returned to help the man called Smoke in his vendetta. Many people *insist* that is the way it happened. That Preacher and Smoke . . .

Well, that's another story.

As the winds changed from cool to cold, and the first flakes of snow touched the valley, Nicole gave birth to a boy.

While Smoke paced the cabin floor, feeling totally inadequate—which, in this situation, he was—a tiny squall of outrage filled the bedroom, as breath was sucked into new lungs. Nicole's hair was stuck to her head from sweaty, painful exertion, and her face was pale.

"Take the knife," she told her husband. "And cut the cord where I show you."

His hand trembled and he hesitated for a second. Her sharp command brought him back.

"Do it, Smoke!"

The umbilical lifeline severed, the baby washed, the tiny wound on his belly bandaged, Nicole wrapped the boy in clean white cloths and the baby nursed at her breast.

"You look like you're going to be sick," Nicole told him. "Go outside."

He did and thought, *what I know about birthing babies would fill volumes. And what I know about the inner strength of women would, too.*

When he again entered the house, Nicole was nursing the child at her breast, and Smoke thought he had never seen a more beautiful sight. He stood in speechless awe.

Fed, warm, and secure, the child then slept beside its mother.

"You sleep, too," Smoke told her. "I'll stand watch."

"If baby Arthur starts to cry," she said wearily, "just take him."

"What am I supposed to *do* with it?"

She smiled at him. "It will come natural to you. Just keep your hand under his head for support."

"Oh, Lord," Smoke said.

Nicole drifted off into sleep and after an hour, the child awakened. With much trepidation, the young man took his son in his big, work-hardened hands and held it gently.

"Now what do I do?" he said.

The baby looked up at him.

"Arthur," Smoke said. "You behave, now."

And the baby, like his namesake, promptly started squalling and grousing.

Winter locked in the valley and Smoke knew, as long as the hard winter held, the three of them would be safe from the stalled pursuit of the bounty hunters. But in the spring, their coming would be inevitable and relentless. Smoke would have to move his family to a safer place.

But where?

His smile was grim. Sure, why not. Right under their noses would be the last place they would look. Idaho. He would have to hang up his .36s—maybe get a new Remington or Colt—carry just one gun. Use Seven for breeding, never for riding. Maybe, he thought, they could pull it off.

Preacher drifted into his mind. God, how he missed that ornery old man, so full of common sense and mountain wisdom. He would have been a great companion for the baby.

Smoke shook his head. But Preacher was gone. And the living have to go on living. Preacher told him that.

He struggled to remember what Preacher had told him about Idaho Territory. He recalled Preacher telling him there was a lake on the eastern pan (Gray's Lake). So wild and beautiful and lonely it had to be seen to be believed. No white men lived there, Preacher said. So that's where Smoke would take his family to live, hopefully, in peace.

But he wondered if he could ever live in peace. And that ever present speculation haunted him, especially when he looked at his wife and son.

If anything ever happened to them . . .

Baby Arthur cooed and gurgled and grew healthy and strong and much loved during the winter of 1871/72. He would be big-boned and strong, with blond hair and blue eyes that flashed when he grew angry.

The three of them waited out the winter, making plans to leave the valley in late spring, when the baby was six months old, and they felt he could stand the trip. They both agreed it would be taking a chance, but one they had to take.

In a settlement that would soon wear the name of Telluride, in the primitive area of the Uncompahgre

Forest, bounty hunters also waited for spring. They were a surly, quarrelsome bunch as the cold days and bitter nights drifted toward spring. With them, a young man who called himself Kid Austin. Kid was quick with a pistol—perhaps the quickest of them all—but the only man he had ever killed was a drunken old Mexican sheepherder. Even with the knowledge that the Kid was untested, the bounty hunters left him alone. For he was uncommonly fast and quick-tempered. And because the man they hunted was a friend of the old mountain man who had humiliated the Kid in front of that saloon, Kid Austin thus hated the man called Smoke. He dreamed of killing this Smoke, of facing him down in a street, beating him to the draw, and watching him die hard in the dirt, crying and begging for mercy, while men stood on the boardwalks and feared him, and women stood and wanted him. Those were his dreams—all his dreams. Kid Austin was not a very imaginative young man. And he would not live to dream many more of his wild dreams of glory and power.

Felter was a patient man, who shared none of the Kid's dreams. Felter didn't know how many white men he had killed. He thought it to be around twenty-five, and nobody gave a damn how many Indians. He slowly spun the cylinder of his Colt. "They got to be in that valley, southwest of the San Juan's. Everything points in that direction."

"That old Ute we talked to," Canning said. "He said something 'bout a blond-haired woman called Little Lightning. That could be Smoke's woman." He grinned. "You boys can have the gunfighter; I'll take me a taste of his wife. I'd like to hump me a yellerhaired white woman. Man gits tired of them greasy squaws."

"You rape all the squaws you take a mind to," a bounty hunter named Grissom told him. "Don't nobody give a damn 'bout them. But you bother a white woman, you gonna get yourself hung."

Canning's grin spread across his unshaven face. "Not ifn I don't leave her alive to talk about it, I won't."

"That there is a thought to think about," Grissom agreed. "But that Ute said she was all swole up with kid, gettin' ready to turn fresh."

"So?"

"What about the kid?"

Canning shrugged that off. "I 'member the time up in north Colorado when we hit an Injun camp—surprised them. That were fun. After we had our fun with some young squaws, I found me a papoose just a-hollerin' and grabbed him up by the heels. Swung him agin a tree. Head popped like a pistol shot."

"That were a Injun kid. This here be a white baby."

"No never-mind. Richards said to kill 'em all. Don't want to leave no youngun around to grow up and git mean."

The bounty hunters all agreed that made sense. And they would pleasure themselves with the woman—then kill her.

"I want Smoke," Kid Austin said. The older bounty hunters smiled. "I want him face on so's I can beat him at his own game. You all just watch me."

"Yeah, Kid," a man called Poker said. "You a real grizzly, you are."

"I just need one chance."

It's probably the only one you'll get, too, Felter

thought. *'Cause if the Preacher took him under his wing and taught him right, this Smoke will be a ring-tailed tooter.*

The first week in April, a violent pre-season thunderstorm, spawned by a week of abnormally warm weather, struck the valley, scattering the herd of breeding horses.

"I've got to get some of them back," Smoke said. "We've got to have them for breeding stock. But I hate to leave you and Little Preacher alone." His face was worry lined, for he knew with the warm weather, the bounty hunters would be riding hard to get him.

She laughed away his fears. "We have to get that cow back for milk, and there is no telling where that fool cow ran off to. And don't forget, I'm a pretty good shot."

"I might be gone for several days."

"Honey," she said touching his face, "it was the hand of Providence that brought us that cow—Lord knows how it got out here. But you've got to get it back for the baby." She pressed a packet of food on him. "I'll be packing while you're finding the herd—and the cow." She laughed. "You always look so serious when you're milking."

"Never *did* like to milk," he said.

He left reluctantly, knowing he had no choice. As he rode away on Seven, he stopped once, turning in the saddle, looking back at his wife, holding their son in her arms. The sun sparkled off her hair, casting a halo of light around the woman and baby. Smoke lifted a hand in goodbye.

Nicole waved at him, then turned and walked back into the cabin.

To the northeast, still many hard miles away, just leaving the last fringes of heavy forest and tall mountains behind them, rode the bounty hunters. Since the middle of March they had fanned out in the mountains, asking questions of any white man and several friendly Indians. The Indians told them nothing, but several white drifters told them of a cabin in the valley, on a knoll, with a little creek running behind it. Where the Delores leaves the San Juans, head southwest, you can't miss it.

Canning's thoughts were of the yellow-haired woman.

Felter thought about the money.

Kid Austin thought of being the man who killed the gunfighter/outlaw Smoke. What a name he'd have after that—and all the women he wanted.

Smoke worked long hours, gathering his precious herd of mustangs and Appaloosa, tucking them in a blind canyon, holding them there while he searched for the others. He found the cow and the old brindle steer that had wandered up with her, probably, Smoke concluded, the only survivors of an Indian attack on a wagon train.

During the late afternoon of the second day out, Smoke thought he heard the faint sounds of gunfire carrying on the wind, blowing from the north, but he could not be certain. He listened intently for several moments. He could hear nothing except the winds, sighing lonely off the far mountains. He returned to his work.

"Fine-lookin' woman," Canning said, looking at Nicole. She was sprawled in semi-awareness on the floor. His eyes lingered on her legs where her dress had slid up when she was knocked to the floor. The bodice of the dress was ripped open, exposing her breasts. Canning licked his lips.

The bounty hunters had destroyed the interior of the cabin, looking for gold that was not there.

One bounty hunter sat in a chair, cursing as he bandaged a bloody arm. "She can shoot," he said. "Damn near tore my arm off. Somebody see ifn you can find a bottle of laudanum."

Felter's eyes found the body of Stoner lying in front of the cabin. "Yeah, she sure can shoot. Just ask Stoner."

"If he answers you," Kid Austin said, "the back door's mine."

They all laughed at this.

"Drag his body out of sight," Felter said. "Don't want to spook this Smoke when he rides up. And hide your horses. We'll take him when he comes in."

Kid Austin opened his mouth to protest.

"Shut up," Felter cut him off. "Maybe you'll get a crack at him, maybe not. I'd like to take him alive, torture him, find out where the gold is."

He knelt down beside Nicole, his hands busy on her body.

Arthur began crying.

"Shut that kid up!" Felter snarled. "'Fore I shoot the little snot."

Canning picked up a blanket and walked to the cradle. He folded the wool and held it over the baby's face for several minutes. The child kicked feebly, then was still as life was smothered from it.

Nicole was stripped naked and shoved into the bedroom. Her hands were tied to the bedposts. Arthur was silent, and Nicole knew, with the awareness mothers seem to possess, her son was dead.

She began weeping.

She opened her eyes, and through the mist of tears, watched Canning drop his trousers to the floor.

The perverted afternoon and evening would wear slowly for Nicole.

And Smoke was a day's ride from the cabin on the knoll in the valley.

THIRTEEN

On the morning of the third day out, Smoke pushed his horses closer to the cabin, a feeling of dread building within him. Some primitive sense of warning caused him to pull up short. He left the cow, the steer, and the horses in a meadow several miles from the cabin.

He made a wide circle of the cabin, staying in the timber back of the creek, and slipped up to the cabin.

Nicole was dead. The acts of the men had grown perverted and in their haste, her throat had been crushed.

Felter sat by the lean-to and watched the valley in front of him. He wondered where Smoke had hidden the gold.

Inside, Canning drew his skinning knife and scalped Nicole, tying her bloody hair to his belt. He then skinned a part of her, thinking he would tan the hide and make himself a nice tobacco pouch.

Kid Austin got sick at his stomach watching Canning's callousness, and went out the back door to puke on the ground. That moment of sickness saved his life—for the time being.

Grissom walked out the front door of the cabin. Smoke's tracks had indicated he had ridden off south, so he would probably return from that direction. But Grissom felt something was wrong. He sensed something; his years on the hoot-owl back trails surfacing.

"Felter?" he called.

"Yeah?" He stepped from the lean-to.

"Something's wrong."

"I feel it. But what?"

"I don't know." Grissom spun as he sensed movement behind him. His right hand dipped for his pistol. Felter had stepped back into the lean-to. Grissom's palm touched the smooth wooden butt of his pistol as his eyes touched the tall young man standing by the corner of the cabin, a Colt .36 in each hand. Lead from the .36s hit him in the center of the chest with numbing force. Just before his heart exploded, the outlaw said, "Smoke!" Then he fell to the ground.

Smoke jerked the gun belt and pistols from the dead man. Remington Army .44s.

A bounty hunter ran from the cabin, firing at the corner of the cabin. But Smoke was gone.

"Behind the house!" Felter yelled, running from the lean-to, his fists full of Colts. He slid to a halt and raced back to the water trough, diving behind its protection.

A bounty hunter who had been dumping his bowels in the outhouse struggled to pull up his pants, at the same time pushing open the door with his shoulder. Smoke shot him twice in the belly and left him to scream on the outhouse floor.

Kid Austin, caught in the open behind the cabin, ran

for the banks of the creek, panic driving his legs. He leaped for the protection of the sandy embankment, twisting in the air, just as Smoke took aim and fired. The ball hit Austin's right buttock and traveled through the left cheek of his butt, tearing out a sizable hunk of flesh. Kid Austin, the dreaming gun-hand, screamed and fainted from the pain in his ass.

Smoke ran for the protection of the woodpile and crouched there, recharging his Colts and checking the .44s. He listened to the sounds of men in panic, firing in all directions, hitting nothing.

Moments ticked past, the sound of silence finally overpowering gunfire. Smoke flicked away sweat from his face. He waited.

Something came sailing out the back door to bounce on the grass. Smoke felt hot bile build in his stomach. Someone had thrown his son outside. The boy had been dead for some time. Smoke fought back sickness.

"You wanna see what's left of your woman?" a taunting voice called from near the back door. "I got her hair on my belt and a piece of her hide to tan. We all took a turn or two with her. I think she liked it."

Smoke felt rage charge through him, but he remained still, crouched behind the thick pile of wood until his rage cooled to controlled venomous-filled fury. He unslung the big Sharps buffalo rifle that Preacher had carried for years. The rifle could drop a two thousand pound buffalo at six hundred yards. It could also punch a hole through a small log.

The voice from the cabin continued to mock and taunt Smoke. But Preacher's training kept him cautious. To his rear lay a meadow, void of cover. To his left was a shed, but he knew that was empty for it was still barred from the outside. The man he'd plugged in the butt was to his right, but several fallen logs would protect him from that direction. The man in the outhouse was either dead or passed out, his screaming had ceased.

Through a chink in the logs, Smoke shoved the muzzle of the Sharps and lined up where he thought he had seen a man move, just to the left of the rear window, to where Smoke had framed it out with rough pine planking. He gently squeezed the trigger, taking up slack. The weapon boomed, the planking shattered, and a man began screaming in pain.

Canning ran out the front of the cabin, to the lean-to, sliding down hard beside Felter behind the water trough. "This ain't workin' out," he panted. "Grissom, Austin, Poker, and now Evans is either dead or dying. The slug from that buffalo gun blowed his arm off. Let's get the hell outta here!"

Felter had been thinking the same thing. "What about Clark and Sam?"

"They growed men. They can join us or they can go to hell."

"Let's ride. They's always another day. We'll hide up in them mountains, see which way he rides out, then bushwhack him. Let's go." They raced for their horses, hidden in a bend of the creek, behind the bank. They kept the cabin between themselves and Smoke as much as possible, then bellied down in the meadow the rest of the way.

In the creek, the water red from the wounds in his butt, Kid Austin crawled upstream, crying in pain and humiliation. His Colts were forgotten—useless anyway; the powder was wet—all he wanted was to get away.

The bounty hunters left in the house, Clark and Sam, looked at each other. "I'm gettin' out!" Sam said. "That ain't no pilgrim out there."

"The hell with that," Clark said. "I humped his woman, I'll kill him and take the eight thousand."

"Your option." Sam slipped out the front and caught up with the others.

Kid Austin reached his horse first. Yelping as he hit the saddle, he galloped off toward the timber in the foothills.

"You wife don't look so good now," Clark called out to Smoke. "Not since she got a haircut and one titty skinned."

Deep silence had replaced gunfire. The air stank of black powder, blood, and relaxed bladders and bowels, death-induced. Smoke had seen the men ride off into the foothills. He wondered how many were left in the cabin.

Smoke remained still, his eyes burning with rage. Smoke's eyes touched the stiffening form of his son. If Clark could have read the man's thoughts, he would have stuck the muzzle of his .44 into his mouth and pulled the trigger, insuring himself a quick death, instead of what waited for him later on.

"Yes, sir," Clark taunted him. He went into profane detail of the rape of Nicole and the perverted acts that followed that.

Smoke eased slowly backward, keeping the woodpile in front of him. He slipped down the side of the knoll and ran around to the side of the small hill, then up it to the side of the cabin. He grinned: The bounty hunter was still talking to the woodpile, to the muzzle of the Sharps stuck through the logs.

Smoke eased around to the front of the cabin and looked in. He saw Nicole, saw the torture marks on her, saw the hideousness of the scalping and the skinning knife. He lifted his eyes to the back door, where Clark was crouching just to the right of the closed door.

Smoke raised his .36 and shot the pistol out of Clark's hand. The outlaw howled and grabbed his numbed and bloodied hand.

Smoke stepped over Grissom's body, then glanced at the body of the armless bounty hunter who had bled to death.

Clark looked up at the tall young man with the burning eyes. Cold slimy fear put a bony hand on his shoulder. For the first time in his evil life, Clark knew what death looked like. "You gonna make it quick, ain't you?"

"Not likely," Smoke said, then kicked him on the side of the head, dropping Clark unconscious to the floor.

When Clark came to his senses, he began screaming. He was naked, staked out a mile from the cabin, on the plain. Rawhide held his wrists and ankles to thick stakes driven into the ground. A huge ant mound was just inches from him. And Smoke had poured honey all over him.

"I'm a white man," Clark screamed. "You can't do this to me." Slobber sprayed from his mouth. "What are you, half Apache?"

Smoke looked at him, contempt in his eyes. "You will not die well, I believe." He mounted Seven and rode back to the cabin.

"Goddamn you!" Clark squalled. He spat out a glob

of honey. "Shoot me, for God's sake! It'll take me days to die like this. You're a devil—you're a devil!"

The ants found him and Clark's screaming was awful in the afternoon.

Smoke blocked the screaming from his mind as he rode back to the cabin, across the plain, so lovely with its profusion of wild flowers. Nicole had loved the wild flowers, he recalled, often picking a bunch of them to brighten a shelf or the table.

By the cabin on the knoll, Smoke found a shovel and began his slow digging of graves, one smaller than the other. Seven would warn him if anyone approached from any direction.

He paused often to wipe the tears from his eyes.

FOURTEEN

Smoke covered the mounds of earth with armloads of wild flowers from the meadow. He asked God to take mother and son into His place of peace and love and beauty.

But Vengeance is Mine, Sayeth the Lord, popped into his brain.

"No, Sir," Smoke said. "Not this time."

Clark's screaming had hoarsened into an animal bellow.

Smoke fashioned two crosses of wood and hammered the stakes into the ground at the head of each grave. He walked down to the creek bank, to the boulder where he had chipped Preacher's name. He added two more names.

Smoke gathered up all the weapons of the dead bounty hunters and put them in the cabin. He had made up his mind to change to the Army .44s. He would pick out the best two later; there would be ample shot and powder. He dragged the bodies of the dead bounty hunters far out into the plain, leaving them for the wolves, the coyotes, and the buzzards, the latter already circling.

It was late afternoon, the dark shadows of blue and purple were deepening. On a ridge to the northeast, Felter watched, as best he could, through field glasses, until it became too dark to see.

"He buried his wife and kid," Felter told the others. "Drug the other bodies out in the plain, buzzards gatherin' now. And he staked out Clark on an anthill."

"The bastard!" Canning cussed.

But Felter chuckled. "He ain't no more bastard than us. He's just tougher than rawhide and meaner than a grizzly, that's all. Madder than hell, too."

Kid Austin moaned in pain.

Felter gazed down into the dark valley. He could not help but feel grudging admiration for the man called Smoke. That would not prevent him from killing Smoke when the time and place presented itself, but it was good to know, at last, what type of man he would be going up against. Felter was one of the best at the quick-draw, but, he reasoned, why tempt fate in that manner when shooting a man in the back was so much safer?

But with this man called Smoke, he pondered, he would have to be very careful how he set up the ambush. For Smoke had been trained by the old mountain man, Preacher, and now Felter knew Smoke was as dangerous as a cornered grizzly. It would not be easy, but it could be done.

The bounty hunters made a cold camp that night. "Look sharp," Felter told the first night guard. "We up against a curly wolf. If any of you doubt that, just listen when the wind changes, and you can hear

Clark squallin'."

No one spoke. They had all heard the howling of Clark. He was dying as hard as if he had been taken by Apache.

The Kid had never seen a man staked out before, but the others had come upon several.

The head would swell to twice its normal size from the ant stings; the eyes would be blind; the genitals would be grotesquely swollen; the lips would be swollen, turned inside out, and the tongue would finally swell up, blacken, and the man would choke to death, usually going insane long before that happened. It usually took two to three days.

Kid Austin shuddered in the night. He lay on his stomach on his blankets. "Smoke's crazy!" he said.

Felter chuckled. "No . . . he's just got a touch of mountain man in him, that's all."

On a mesa opposite the timber where Felter and the others slept, Smoke made his cold camp. Seven was on guard. Sleep finally took the young man in soft arms . . . almost as soft as the arms of Nicole.

And he dreamed of her, and of their son.

Long before first light touched the mountains and the valley, creating that morning's panorama of color, Smoke was up and moving. He rode across the valley. Stopping out of range of rifles, by a stand of cottonwoods, he calmly and arrogantly built a cook fire. He put on coffee to boil and sliced bacon into a pan. He speared out the bacon and dropped slices of potatoes into the grease, frying them crisp. With hot coffee and hot food, and a hunk of Nicole's fresh baked bread, Smoke settled down for a leisurely breakfast. He knew the outlaws were watching him; had seen the sun glint off glass yesterday afternoon.

"That bastard!" Canning cussed him.

But Felter again had to chuckle. "Relax. He's just tryin' to make us do something stupid. Stay put."

"I'd like to go down there and call him out," Kid said. His bravado had returned from his sucking on the laudanum bottle all night.

Felter almost told him to go ahead, get the rest of his butt shot off.

"You just stay put," he told Austin. "Rest your butt. We got time. They's just one of him, four of us."

"They was twice that yesterday," Sam reminded him.

Felter said nothing in rebuttal.

The valley upon which the outlaws gazed, and upon which Smoke was eating his quiet breakfast, as Seven munched on young spring grass, was wild in its grandeur. It was several miles wide, many miles long, with rugged peaks on the north end, far in the distance, snow covered most of the time, with thick forests. And, Smoke smiled grimly, many deadend canyons. One of which was only a few miles from this spot. And he felt sure the bounty hunters did not know it was a box, for it looked very deceiving.

Clark had told Smoke, in the hopes he would only get a bullet in the head, not ants on the brain, that it was Canning who scalped his wife, Canning who first raped her, Canning who skinned her breast to make a tobacco pouch with the tanned hide.

Smoke cleaned up his skillet and plate and then set about checking out the two Remington .44s he had chosen from the pile of guns. Preacher had been after him for several years to switch, and Smoke had fired and handled Preacher's Remington .44 many times, liking the feel of the weapon, the balance. And he was just as fast with the slightly heavier weapon.

He spent an hour or more rigging holsters for his new guns, then spent a few minutes drawing and firing them. To his surprise, he found the weapon, with its sleeker form and more laid-back hammer, increased his speed.

His smile was not pleasant. For he had plans for Canning.

Mounting up, he rode slowly to the northeast, always keeping out of rifle range, and very wary of any ambush. When Smoke disappeared into the timber, Felter made his move.

"Let's ride," he said. "Let's get the hell out of here."

But after several hours, Felter realized *they* were being pushed toward the northwest. Every time they tried to veer off, a shot from the big Sharps would keep them going.

On the second day, Canning brought his horse up sharply, hurting the animal's mouth with the bit. "I 'bout had this," he said.

They were tired and hungry, for Smoke had harassed them with the Sharps every hour.

Felter looked around him, at the high walls of the canyon, sloping upward, green and brown with timber. He smiled ruefully. *They* were now the hunted.

A dozen times in the past two days they had tried to bushwhack Smoke. But he was as elusive as his name.

"Somebody better do something," Felter said. "'Cause we're in a box canyon."

"I'll take him!" Canning snarled. "Rest of you ride on up 'bout a mile or two. Get set in case I miss." He grinned. "But I ain't gonna do that, boys."

Felter nodded. "See you in a couple of hours."

Smoke had dismounted just inside the box canyon, ground reining Seven. Smoke removed his boots and slipped on moccasins. Then he went on the prowl, as silent as death. He held a skinning knife in his left hand.

"No shots," Austin said. "And it's been three hours."

Sam sat quietly. Everything about this job had turned sour.

"Horse comin'," Felter said.

"There he is!" Austin said. "And it's Canning. By God, he said he'd get him, and he did."

But Felter wasn't sure about that. He'd smelled wood smoke about an hour back. That didn't fit any pattern. And Canning wasn't sitting his horse right. Then the screaming drifted to them. Canning was hollering in agony.

"What's he hollerin' for?" Kid asked. "I hurt a lot more'un anything he could have wrong with him."

"Don't bet on that," Felter told him. He scrambled down the gravel and brush-covered slope to halt Canning's frightened horse.

Felter recoiled in horror at the sight of Canning's blood-soaked crotch.

"My privates!" Canning squalled. "Smoke waylaid me and gelded me! He cauterized me with a runnin' iron." Canning passed out, tumbling from the saddle.

Felter and Sam dragged the man into the brush and

looked at the awful wound. Smoke had heated a running iron and seared the wound, stopping most of the bleeding. Felter thought Canning would live, but his raping days were over.

And Felter knew, with a sudden realization, that he wanted no more of the man called Smoke. Not without about twenty men backing him up, that is.

Using a spare shirt from his saddlebags, Felter made a crude bandage for Canning. But it was going to be hell on the man sitting a saddle. He looked around him. That fool Kid Austin was walking down the floor of the canyon, his hands poised over his twin Colts. An empty laudanum bottle lay on the ground.

"Get back here, you fool!" Felter shouted.

Austin ignored him. "Come on, Smoke!" he yelled. "I'm goin' to kill you."

"Hell with you, Kid," Sam muttered.

They tied Canning in the saddle and rode off, up the slope of the canyon wall, high up, near the crest. There they found a hole that just might get them free. Raking their horses's sides, the animals fought for footing, digging and sliding in the loose rock. The horses realized they had to make it—or die. With one final lunge, the horses cleared the crest and stood on firm ground, trembling from fear and exhaustion.

As they rested the animals, they looked for the Kid. Austin was lost from sight.

They rode off to the north, toward a mining camp where Richards had said he would leave word, or send more men should this crew fail.

Well, Felter reflected bitterly, we damn sure failed.

Austin, his horse forgotten, his mind numbed by overdoses of laudanum, stumbled down the rocky floor of the canyon, screaming and cursing Smoke. He pulled up short when he spotted his quarry.

Smoke sat calmly on a huge rock, munching on a cold biscuit.

"Get up!" the Kid shouted. "Get on your feet and face me like a man oughtta."

Smoke finished his meager meal, then rose to his feet. He was smiling.

Kid Austin walked on, narrowing the distance, finally stopping about thirty feet from Smoke. "I'll be known as the man who killed Smoke," he said. "Me! Kid Austin."

Smoke laughed at him.

The Kid flushed. "I done it to your wife, too, Jensen. She liked it so much she asked me to do it to 'er some more. So I obliged 'er. I took your woman, now I'm gonna take you." He dipped his right hand downward.

Smoke drew his right hand .44 with blinding speed, drawing, cocking, firing, before Austin could realize what was taking place in front of his eyes. The would-be gunfighter felt two lead fists of pain strike him in the belly, one below his belt buckle, the other just above the ornate silver buckle. The hammerlike blows dropped him to his knees. Hurt began creeping into his groin and stomach. He tried to pull his guns from leather, but his hands would not respond to the commands from his brain.

"I'm Kid Austin," he managed to say. "You can't do this to me."

"Looks like I did, though," Smoke said. He turned away from the dying man and walked back to Seven, swinging into the saddle. He rode off without looking back.

"Momma!" the Kid called, as the pain in his belly grew more intense. "It hurts, Momma. Help me."

But only the animals and the canyon heard his cries for help. They alone witnessed his begging. The clop of Seven's hooves grew fainter.

His intestines mangled, one kidney shattered, and his spleen ruptured, the Kid died on his knees in the rocky canyon, in a vague praying position. He remained that way for a long time, until his horse picked up its master's scent and found him, nudging him with its nose, toppling the Kid over on his side. The horse bolted from the blood smell, running down the canyon. One Colt fell from a holster, clattering on the rocks, to shine in the thin sunlight filtering through the timber of the narrow canyon.

Then the canyon was quiet, with only the sighing of the wind.

Smoke rode back to the cabin in the valley and packed his belongings, covering the pack frame with a ground sheet. He rubbed Seven down and fed him grain and hay, stabling him in the lean-to.

He cleaned his guns and made camp outside the cabin. He could not bear to sleep inside that house of death and torture and rape. His sleep was restless during those starry nights of the first week back in the valley; his sleep troubled by nightmares of Nicole calling out his name, of the baby's dying.

The second week was no better, his sleep interrupted by the same nightmares. So when he kicked out of his blankets on this final morning in the valley, his body covered with sweat, Smoke knew he would never rest well until the men who were responsible for this tragedy were dead—Potter, Stratton, Richards.

Smoke bathed in the creek, doing so quickly, for the creek and the mossy bank also held memories. He saddled Seven and cinched the pack on a pack horse, then went to the graves by the cabin, hat in hand, to visit with his wife and son.

"I don't know that I will ever return," he spoke quietly. "I wish it could have been different, Nicole. I wish we could have lived out our lives in peace, together, raising our family. I wish a lot of things, Nicole. Goodbye."

With tears in his eyes, he mounted Seven and rode away, pointing the nose of the big spotted horse north.

But in a settlement on the banks of the Uncompahgre, Felter and Sam and Canning were telling a much different version of what happened in the cabin in the valley.

FIFTEEN

"I'm tellin' you boys," Felter said to the miners, "I ain't never seen nothin' like it. Them murderin' Utes raped the woman, killed her and the baby, then scalped 'em. It was terrible."

"Yeah," Sam picked up the lie. "Then that outlaw, Smoke Jensen, he all of a sudden comes up on us—shootin'. He kilt Grissom and Poker and Evans right off. Just shot 'em dead for no reason. He went crazy, I guess. Stampeded our horses and Felter and me took cover in a waller. He took our horses."

"Time we worked our way out," Felter said, "this Smoke had killed the rest of our crew and staked out Clark on an anthill, stripped him neked and poured honey all over him." He hung his head in sorrow. "Wasn't nothin' we could do for him. You boys know how hard a man dies like that."

The miners listened quietly.

"I found Canning," Felter said. "You all know what was done to him. Most awfullest thing I ever seen one white man do to another. Kid Austin was shot in the back; never even had a chance to pull his guns."

Some of the miners believed Felter; most did not. They knew about Smoke, the stories told, and knew about Felter and his scummy crew. Some of them had known Preacher, and knew the mountain man would not take a murderer to raise as his son. The general consensus was that Felter and Sam and Canning were lying.

Felter had not told them of the men riding hard toward the camp; men sent by Richards and Stratton and Potter. That message was waiting for Felter when he arrived at the miners' camp.

Several miners left the smoke-filled tent, to gather in the dusky coolness.

"Pass the word," one said. "This boy Smoke is bein' set up. We all know the story as to why."

"Yeah. The fight'll be lopsided, but I sure don't wanna miss it. I hear tell this Smoke is poison with a short gun."

"Myself. See you."

Although the trail of Felter was three weeks old, it was not that difficult to follow: a bloody bandage from Canning's wounds; a carelessly doused campfire; an empty bottle of laudanum and several pints of whiskey. And Indians told him of sighting the men.

It all pointed toward the silver camp near the Uncompahgre. And it also meant Felter was probably expecting more men to join him—probably more men than had attacked his cabin. How many brave men does it take to rape and kill one woman and a baby?

That thought lay bitter on his mind as he rode, following the trail with dogged determination.

Just south of what would soon be named Telluride, in the gray granite mountains, two miners stopped the young man on the spotted horse—stopped him warily.

"I was told you'd be ridin' a big spotted horse with a mean look in its eyes," a miner said. "I ain't tryin' to be nosy, young feller, but if you're the man called Smoke, I got news."

"I'm Smoke." He took out tobacco and paper and rolled a cigarette, handing the makings to the miners.

"Thanks," one said, after they had all rolled, licked, and lit. "'Bout fourteen salty ol' boys waitin' for you at the silver camp. Most of us figure Felter lied 'bout what happened at your cabin. What did happen?"

Smoke told them, leaving nothing out.

"That's 'bout the way we had it figured. Son, you can't go up agin all them folks—no matter how you feel. That'd be foolish. They's too many."

"If they're gun-hands for Potter or Richards or Stratton, I intend to kill them."

"'Pears to me, son, they 'bout wiped out your whole family."

"They made just one mistake," Smoke said.

"What's that?"

"They left me alive."

The miners had nothing to say to that.

"Thanks for the information." Smoke moved out.

The miners watched him leave. One said, "I wouldn't miss this for nothin'. This here is gonna be a fight that'll be yakked about for a hundred years to come. You can tell your grandkids 'bout this. Providin', that is, you can find a woman to live with your ugly face."

"Thank you. But you ain't no rose. Come on."

How the tall young man had managed to Injun up on him, the miner didn't know. He was woods-wise and yet he hadn't heard a twig snap or a leaf rustle. Just that sudden cold sensation of a rifle muzzle pressing against his neck.

"My name is Smoke."

The miner almost ruined a perfectly good pair of long johns.

"If you got friends in that camp," Smoke told him, "you go down and very quietly tell them to ease out. 'Cause in one hour, I'm opening this dance."

"My name is Big Jake Johnson, Mr. Smoke—and I'm on your side."

Smoke removed the muzzle from the man's neck.

"Thank you," the miner said.

"Do it without alarming Felter and his crew."

"Consider it done. But Smoke, they's fourteen hardcases in that camp. And they're waitin' for you."

"They won't have long to wait."

The mining camp, one long street, with tents and rough shacks on both sides of the dusty street, looked deserted as Smoke gazed down from his position on the side of a sloping canyon wall.

The miners had left the camp, retreating to a spot on the northwest side of the canyon. They would have a grandstand view of the fight.

Felter knew what was happening seconds after the miners began leaving, and began positioning his men around the shacky camp.

The owners of the two saloons had wrestled kegs of beer and bottles of whiskey up the side of the hill, and were now doing a thriving business. A party atmosphere prevailed. This was better than a hanging—lasted longer, and would have a lot more action. But when the first shot was fired, the miners and the barkeeps would head for pre-picked out boulders and trees. Watching a good gunfight was one thing; getting shot was quite another.

"Felter!" Smoke called, his voice rolling down the hillside. "You and Canning want to settle this between us? I'll meet you both—stand-up, two to one. How about it?"

In a shack, an outlaw known only as Lefty looked at Felter. "You ain't never gonna take this one alive, Felter. No way."

Felter nodded. "I know it." He was crouched behind a huge packing crate. No one in his right mind would trust the thin walls to protect him. A Henry .44 could punch through four inches of pine.

"Give us the gold your Daddy stole!" Felter yelled. "Then you just ride on out of here."

"My Pa didn't steal any gold. He just took what your bosses stole from the South—after they murdered my brother. And I don't have it," Smoke said truthfully.

Smoke shifted positions, slipping about twenty-five yards to his right. He had seen a man dart from the camp, working his way up the side of the hill.

Smoke watched the man pause and get set for a shot.

He raised the Henry and put a slug in the man's belly, slamming him backward. The man screamed, dropped his rifle, and tumbled down the embankment, rolling and clawing on his way down. He landed in a sprawl in the street, struggling to get to his feet. Smoke shot him in the chest and he fell forward. He did not move.

The miners across the way cheered and hollered.

"Thirteen to go," Smoke muttered. He again shifted positions, grabbing up the dead man's Henry, shucking the cartridges from it, putting them in his pocket.

Smoke watched as men fanned out in the town, moving too quickly for him to get a shot. Just to keep them jumpy, Smoke put a round in back of one man's boots. The man yelped and dived for the protection of a shack.

"You boys ridin' with Felter!" Smoke yelled. "You sure you want to stay with this dance? The music's gonna get mighty fierce in a minute."

"You go to hell!" the voice came from a shack. A dozen other voices shouted curses at Smoke.

Two men sprang from behind a building, rifles in their hands. They raced into a shack. Smoke put ten .44 rounds into the shack, working his Henry from left to right, waist high.

One man screamed and stumbled out into the street, dropping his rifle. He died in the dirt, boot heels drumming out his death song. The second man staggered out, his chest and belly crimson. He sat down in the street, remained that way for a moment, then toppled over on his face.

Smoke shifted positions once more, reloaded, and called out, "Anymore of you boys want to dance to my music?"

Canning looked at Felter, both of them crouched behind the packing crate. "Hell with the gold. I'll settle for the eight thousand. Let's rush him."

Felter was thoughtful for a moment. This whole plan was screwed up; nothing had worked right from the beginning. Smoke was pure devil—right out of hell. The cabin they had searched had been clean, but poor in worldly goods. Smoke didn't have the gold. For all Felter knew, his Pa might have spent it on whiskey and whores.

Felter knew only that he could not fail twice. He could never set foot in the Idaho Territory if he botched this job, and the way it looked, it was going to be another screw-up.

"All right," he said to Canning. "Can you ride?"

"I'll do anything just so's I can take him alive; so's I can use my knife on him. Listen to him scream."

Felter doubted Smoke would give any man the pleasure of screaming. But he kept that thought to himself. He also kept other thoughts to himself. He was sorry he ever got mixed up in this, and for the first time he could recall, he knew fear. For the first time in his evil life, Felter was really afraid of another man.

"All right," Felter said. "This time, by God, let's take him."

He passed his orders down the street, from shack to shack. Three men to the right, three men to the left, three to stay in town, and two to circle around Smoke, coming in from the rear.

But Smoke had other ideas, and he was putting them into play. His guns roared, a man screamed.

"Damnit, Felter!" Lefty yelled, running across the dusty street. "The hombre's in *town*!"

Smoke's .44s thundered. Lefty spun in the street, a cry pushing out of his throat as twin spots of red appeared on his shirt front. He stumbled to the dirt.

"I'll kill him!" a short hairy man snarled, running down the side of the street, darting in and out of doorways. He was shooting at everything he thought he saw.

"Over here," Smoke called.

The outlaw spun and Smoke pulled both triggers of a shotgun he removed from under the counter of a tent saloon. The blast lifted the man off his feet, almost cutting him in half.

Smoke reloaded the sawed-off as he ducked down an alley, behind a shack, and up that alley. He came face to face with an ugly bounty hunter. The bounty hunter fired, the lead creasing Smoke's left arm, drawing blood. Smoke pulled the triggers of the sawed-off and blew the man's head from his shoulders.

He stepped into an open door just as a man ran toward him, his fists full of .45s. Splinters from the door frame jabbed painfully into Smoke's cheek as he dropped the shotgun and grabbed his .44s. He shot the man in the chest and belly, the bounty hunter falling into a water trough. He tried to lift a .45 and Smoke shot him between the eyes at a distance no more than five feet. The trough became colored with red and gray.

The street erupted in black powder, whining lead, and wild cursing. Horses broke from their hitch-rails and charged wild-eyed up and down the street, clouding the air with dust, rearing and screaming in fear.

Smoke felt a hot sear of pain in his right leg. The leg

buckled. He flung himself out of the doorway and to the protection of the trough as Canning hobbled painfully into the street, his hands full of guns, belching smoke and flame, his eyes wild with hate.

One of Canning's slugs hit Smoke in the left side, passing through the fleshy part and exiting out the back as he knelt on his knees, firing. The shock spun him around and knocked him down. Smoke raised up on one elbow and leveled a .44, taking careful aim. He shot Canning in the right eye, taking off part of his face. Canning's legs jerked out from under him and he fell on his back, his left eye open and staring in disbelief.

Smoke jerked pistols from the headless outlaw's belt and hand just as Sam and another man ran into the smoky, dusty street, trying to find a target through the din and the haze. Smoke fired at them just as they found him and began shooting. A slug ricocheted off a rock in the street, part of the lead hitting Smoke in the chest, bringing blood and a grunt of pain.

Smoke dragged himself into an alleyway and quickly reloaded all four .44s. He was bleeding from wounds in his side, his leg, his face, and his chest, but he was also mad as hell. He looked around for a target, shoving the fully loaded spare .44s behind his belt.

Sam was on his knees in the middle of the street, one arm broken by a .44 slug. The outlaw screamed curses at Smoke and lifted a pistol, the hammer back. Smoke shot him in the chest. Sam jerked but refused to die. He pulled the trigger of his pistol, the lead plowing up the street and enveloping the man in dust. Smoke shot him again, in the belly. Sam doubled over, dropping his pistol. He died in the center of the street, in a bowing position, his head resting on the dirt, his hat blowing away as a gust of wind whipped between the tents and shacks.

Lead began whining down the alley, and Smoke limped and ran behind a building, pausing to reload and to catch his breath. It has been said that it's hard to stop a man who knows he's in the right and just keeps on coming. Smoke knew he was right—and he kept on coming.

Another of Felter's men ran across the street and down the dirt walkway and into the open alleyway just as Smoke stepped away from the building.

Smoke shot him twice in the belly and kept on coming.

The miners were shouting and cheering and betting on who would be the last man on his feet when the fight was over. Bets against Smoke were getting hard to place.

Sam's partner stepped out and called to Smoke, firing as he yelled. One slug spun Smoke around as it struck the handle of a .44 stuck behind his belt. Pain doubled him over for a second. He lifted his Remingtons and dropped the man to the dirt.

The sounds of a horse galloping hard away came to Smoke as Felter's last man still on his feet ran out of a shack behind Smoke. Smoke coolly lifted a .44 and shot him six times, duckwalking the man across the street, the slugs sending dust popping from the man's shirt front with each impact.

It was almost over.

Smoke reloaded his Remingtons, dropped the spare .44s to the dirt, and took a deep breath, feeling a twinge of pain from at least one broken rib, maybe two.

Felter had sat behind kegs of beer in the tent saloon

and watched it all. He had had a dozen or more opportunities to shoot Smoke from ambush—but he could not bring himself to do it. Jensen was just too much of a man for that. He poured himself a glass of whiskey and shook his head.

What he had seen was the stuff legends are made of; it was rare—but it was not unknown to the West for one man to take on impossible odds and win.

He stood up. "I believe I can take you now, Smoke," he muttered. "You got to be runnin' out of steam."

"Felter!" Smoke called. "Step out here and face me." Blood dripped from his wounds to plop in the dust. His face was bloody and blood and sweat stained his clothing.

Smoke carefully wiped his hands free of sweat just as Felter stepped out of the tent saloon. Both men's guns were in leather. Felter held a shot glass full of whiskey in his left hand. Smoke's right thumb was hooked behind his gun-belt, just over the buckle. Twenty-five feet separated them when Felter stopped. The miners were silent, almost breathless on the hillside, watching this last showdown—for one of the men.

"I seen it, but it's tough for me to believe. You played hell with my men."

Smoke said nothing.

"You and me, now, huh, kid?"

"That's it, and then I take out your bosses."

Felter laughed at him and sipped his whiskey. "I just don't think you can beat me, kid."

"One way to find out."

"I think you're scared, Smoke."

"I'm not afraid of you or of any other man on the

face of this earth."

His words chilled the outlaw. He mentally shook away that damnable edge of fear that touched him.

Felter drained the shot glass. Whiskey and blood would be the last thing he would taste on this earth. "Your wife sure looked pretty neked."

Smoke's grin was ugly. "I'm glad you think so, Felter—'cause you'll never see another woman."

Felter flushed. Damn the man's eyes! he thought. I can't make him mad. "You ready, Smoke?"

"Anytime."

Felter braced himself. "Now!"

The air blurred in front of Felter, then filled with the thunderous roar of gunfire and black smoke. The bounty hunter was on his feet, but something was very wrong. There was something pressing against his back. He felt with his hands. A hitch-rail.

Empty hands! Empty?

My hands can't be empty, he thought. "What . . . ?" he managed to say. Then the shock of his wounds hit him hard.

Why . . . I didn't even clear leather, he thought. The damn kid pulled a cross-draw and beat me! Me!

Felter steadied his eyes to see if he could be wrong. Smoke's left hand holster was empty. He watched the kid shove the .44 back into leather.

"No way!" Felter said. He reached for his Colt and lifted it. His movements seemed so slow. He jacked back the hammer and something blurred in front of him.

Then the sound reached his ears and the fury of the slug in his stomach brought a scream from his lips.

Felter again lifted his Colt and a booming blow struck him on the breastbone, somersaulting him over the hitch-rail, to land on his backside under the striped pole of a tent barber shop.

But Felter was a tough, barrel-chested man, and would not die easily. Unable to rise, he struggled to pull his left hand Colt. He managed to get the pistol up, hammer back, and pointed. Then Smoke's .44 roared one more time, the slug hitting Felter in the jaw, taking off most of the outlaw's face. The slug whined off bone and hit the striped barber pole, spinning it.

The street was quiet. The battle was over.

The barber pole squeaked and turned, then was silent.

Smoke sank to his knees in the dirt.

"You hard hit, son," a miner told him. Unnecessary information, for Smoke knew he was hurt. "You can't just ride out bleedin' like that."

Smoke swung into the saddle, gathering the reins in his left hand, the pack horse rope in his right. "I'll be all right."

He had cleaned his wounds in town, now he wanted the high country, where he would make poultices of herbs and wild flowers, as Preacher had taught him.

The mountain man's words returned to him. "Nature's way is the best, son. You let old Mother Nature take care of you. They's a whole medicine chest right out there in that field. All a man's gotta do is learn 'em."

"When you boys plant them," Smoke told the crowd,

"put on their headboards that Smoke Jensen was right and they were wrong."

He rode off to the west.

"Boys," a miner said. "We just seen us a livin' legend. You remember his name, 'cause we all gonna be hearin' a lot more about that young feller."

EPILOGUE

For a month Smoke tended to his wounds and rested at his camp on the banks of the San Miguel, on the west side of the Uncompahgre Forest. He rested and treated his wounds with poultices.

He ate well of venison, fished in the river, and made stews of wild potatoes and onions and rabbit and squirrel. He slept twelve to fifteen hours a day, feeling his strength slowly returning to him. And he dreamed his dreams of Nicole, her soft arms soothing him, melting away the hurt and fever, calming his sleep, loving him back to health.

At the beginning of the fifth week, he knew he was ready to ride, ready to move, and he carefully checked his guns, cleaning them, rubbing oil into the pockets of his holsters, until the deadly .44s fitted in and out smoothly.

Then he packed his gear and rode out.

In the southwestern corner of Wyoming, a wanted poster tacked to a tree brought him up short.

WANTED
DEAD OR ALIVE
THE OUTLAW AND MURDERER
SMOKE JENSEN
10,000.00 REWARD
Contact the Sheriff at Bury, Idaho Territory

Smoke removed the wanted flyer and carefully folded it, tucking it in his pocket. He looked up to watch an eagle soar high above him, gliding majestically north-westward.

"Take a message with you, eagle," Smoke said. "Tell Potter and Richards and Stratton and all their gunhands I'm coming to kill them. For my Pa, for Preacher, for my son, and for making me an outlaw. And they'll die just as hard as Nicole did. You tell them, eagle. I'm coming after them."

The eagle dipped its wings and flew on.

ASHES

by William W. Johnstone

OUT OF THE ASHES (1137, $3.50)

Ben Raines hadn't looked forward to the War, but he knew it was coming. After the balloons went up, Ben was one of the survivors, fighting his way across the country, searching for his family, and leading a band of new pioneers attempting to bring American OUT OF THE ASHES.

FIRE IN THE ASHES (2669, $3.95)

It's 1999 and the world as we know it no longer exists. Ben Raines, leader of the Resistance, must regroup his rebels and prep them for bloody guerrilla war. But are they ready to face an even fiercer foe—the human mutants threatening to overpower the world!

ANARCHY IN THE ASHES (2592, $3.95)

Out of the smoldering nuclear wreckage of World War III, Ben Raines has emerged as the strong leader the Resistance needs When Sam Hartline, the mercenary, joins forces with an invading army of Russians, Ben and his people raise a bloody banner of defiance to defend earth's last bastion of freedom.

SMOKE FROM THE ASHES (2191, $3.50)

Swarming across America's Southern tier march the avenging soldiers of Libyan blood terrorist Khamsin. Lurking in the blackened ruins of once-great cities are the mutant Night People, crazed killers of all who dare enter their domain. Only Ben Raines, his son Buddy, and a handful of Ben's Rebel Army remain to strike a blow for the survival of America and the future of the free world!

ALONE IN THE ASHES (2591, $3.95)

In this hellish new world there are human animals and Ben Raines—famed soldier and survival expert—soon becomes their hunted prey. He desperately tries to stay one step ahead of death, but no one can survive ALONE IN THE ASHES.